T0243271

YAZOO CLAY

Schuyler Dickson

Tartt Fiction Award

Livingston Press

The University of West Alabama

Copyright © 2022 Schuyler Dickson
All rights reserved, including electronic text
ISBN 13: 978-1-60489-322-9, hardcover
ISBN 13: 978-1-60489-321-2, trade paper
ISBN 13: 978-1-60489-323-6, e-book
Library of Congress Control Number 2022935861
Printed on acid-free paper.
Printed in the United States of America by
Publishers Graphics
Hardcover binding by: Heckman Bindery
Typesetting and page layout: Cassidy Pedram
Proofreading: Christin Loehr, Keneshia Cook,
Cassidy Pedram, Brooke Barger
Cover art: Carol Cruz
Cover Design and Layout: Schuyler Dickson, McKenna Darley
Author photo: Jane Oliver Dickson

This is a work of fiction. Any resemblance
to persons living or dead is coincidental.
Livingston Press is part of The University of West Alabama,
and thereby has non-profit status.
Donations are tax-deductible.

first edition
6 5 4 3 2 1

YAZOO CLAY

STORIES

For Jane Oliver

Table of Contents

HAPPY BIRTHDAY

Before the rain came, Clyde drove to the bridge and fished. He cast three lines and leaned the poles up against the concrete railing and sat on the back of his tailgate, watching the lines and reading the graffiti and listening to the cows in the pasture nearby.

It had been raining almost every day, and each afternoon he'd come home with buckets full of catfish that he would clean and cut into fillets and drop into gallon-sized plastic bags that he would store in the freezer in the kitchen. It got to where his freezer would hardly close it was so packed with fish.

On Sundays—after working all night at the furniture plant where he swept floors and emptied trashcans—Clyde fished all morning and slept all afternoon. He woke up in the evening and drank a beer and heated a couple of inches of oil in a big pan and he fried catfish and hush puppies and French fries. He and his daughter, Becca, ate and watched the rain fall in big drops and pool in the yard in puddles that rose and rose.

Becca was always on her phone unless she hit her data limit, and then she would sulk around the house or read a magazine and breathe out the loudest, boredest sigh anyone had ever heard. She was thirteen.

"I've got to get out of this house," she said, lying sideways across the chair.

"Unless you got a boat," Clyde said, "you ain't going nowhere. The water's up over the road. Almost up to the mailbox. Even if you're a piece of mail you're not going nowhere."

"Ugh," she said. "This is so stupid."

His daughter was starting to become a mystery to him. Every month, she changed into a different being: new clothes that he hadn't bought, shinier, smaller. She spent untold hours poking her lips out at her phone and taking pictures of herself, only to edit the picture so much that the picture looked like a stranger. He loved her, and the way he tried to express his love was by trying not to control her. By leaving her alone.

Outside, the wind began to bend the limbs of the tall trees, sweeping leaves and dust in clouds across the ground. The power flickered and went out. Clyde put on his raincoat and stepped out into the storm and got a small generator from the shed. He dragged the generator inside and started it with a little trouble and plugged the freezer and refrigerator in.

"Can't I plug in my phone?" Becca said.

"You can't eat your phone," he said as the trailer swayed in the heavy wind. Keeping the freezer going meant he would always have food, and always having food meant that, no matter what, he would never be wholly subject to another man. Nothing could touch him. "Here." He took his phone and propped it against a half-empty beer can on the coffee table. "We can watch the news if you want."

"No one watches the news," she said.

On his small screen, a meteorologist stood in his suit and his suspenders and pointed at a green mass as it swept across the area. Yellow circles swarmed and swirled around notches of the storm where wind speeds and cones stretched out among cartoon-like lightning bolts.

Clyde fell asleep watching. He woke at noon the next day and plugged the coffee maker into the generator and as the coffee dripped he looked out the window above the kitchen sink where, outside, the water had risen. The whole road was flooded. The pasture across the road, too. Cows stood huddled on a small hill.

"Becca," he said, thinking to wake her up to show her the cows. She always got a kick out of the cows. "Becca," he said again, but she wasn't on the couch.

Her phone was sitting on the table.

He walked down the small, dark hallway and pushed open

Schuyler Dickson

her cracked door. "Hey, Becca," he said. "Check out them cows."

But she wasn't in her bed. He opened the curtains and gray light spilled in. The bed was empty.

The bathroom was empty, too.

He looked back out the window above the kitchen sink. His truck was there. She hadn't stolen it. Water was over halfway up the tires.

He drank coffee with the windows open until the coffee was gone, and then he made another pot. By afternoon, the sun came out, and all Clyde could hear was the stillness of the wind rippling across the water. His heart thumped as he tried to imagine Becca swimming away. Where would she go? Where was there to go?

There, in the quiet, Clyde felt the roaring, gurgling flood of his insides. It was always there—something to be embarrassed about, like walking around with a bone protruding out of an arm or a hook sticking out of his mouth—and if he sat around too long without casting a line or running his floor sweeper, it would feel as if the current of rage and disappointment would consume not just him but his house and his life and all the known world.

To distract himself, he considered that Becca had been abducted by aliens. He had to admit that it was possible. And maybe as a way to distance himself from the dark images that popped up in his mind when he thought about where she might be, maybe as a way to deal with solitude, he did what he trained himself to do to keep the dark whirlpool from eating him whole: he constructed fantasies.

First, if she were to be abducted by aliens, he would be upset, worried about Becca's safety. Was she terrified? Did the aliens administer something to her that made her freeze, emotionally and physically, and did the inability to feel pain or express terror somehow amplify the pain and terror by silencing their ability to be expressed? And after that had passed—the worry for her—what was he to do with the jealousy that aliens had chosen to take her and not him?

And, further, why was it that some beings abduct and some beings possess? And how often did beings get both abducted and possessed? Like for instance Clyde's spirit: maybe his spirit was abducted and in its place the turning whirlpool of anger and rage had possessed him? But wasn't the whole point of possession to whisper directives?

Not one directive had ever been whispered to Clyde. No direction, no order. No alien whispers or tracking devices. Only the swirling and the skin.

His phone rang. His manager, Mark, was calling.

"Yeah," Clyde said.

"Clyde?" Mark said as if anyone else had ever answered Clyde's phone but Clyde.

"Yeah."

"You staying dry?"

Clyde looked at the window at the water. "Mostly."

"Look, man. You been by the factory today?"

"There's water up over my tires. There's no going nowhere."

"The factory's flooded. All this rain, man. It's everywhere."

"You need me to come clean it."

"I mean it's flooded flooded. The machines, man. We haven't gotten a damage assessment but the whole damn place is wet. Like wet wet."

"Oh. Wow."

"Yeah. I mean, we'll know more I guess once the water recedes and all that. But there ain't no making furniture in a flooded factory. You know what I mean?"

"Yeah. I know what you mean."

"We're not gonna be working for a while, I guess is what I'm trying to say. I'm not sure if it's ever going to open back up. You get what I'm saying?"

"Yeah."

"I'm sorry, man."

"No, I'm sorry."

"Hey, bud. You okay?"

He looked out at the water again. It was just sitting there. "Yeah, I'm fine. Are you fine?"

Mark laughed. "Don't you worry about me, buddy. Look, I'll holler at you later once we get more news. I've got a bunch more phone calls to make."

"Yeah. Okay."

"You go down to the bridge yesterday morning?"

"Yeah."

"You catch anything?"

"I caught some, yeah. I'm running out of room in my freezer."

Mark laughed again. "That a boy. Let me make these calls. I'll holler at you later."

"Okay."

He hung up the phone and imagined the factory under water. How strange it must look, how beautiful.

Two contradictory emotions began to swirl in him. The first was freedom. Clyde was pretty sure that he didn't have a job anymore. He liked having a job, liked having something to do, liked having a paycheck coming in, but he didn't like the hierarchy of having someone over him. And now, without a job, he was without a hierarchy. That felt like freedom.

The second was dread. He needed money. Maybe he didn't need gas, because nowhere was really worth going to. Beer was nice but he had done without it before. He could catch his own food from the creek. He heard the generator whirring. He needed money to keep the freezer running. He needed money to keep Becca's phone on. That was important to her.

He picked up her dead phone and found a charger and plugged the phone and charger into the generator. He wished she were here. For some reason, he had the urge to take her to the factory so they could see what it looked like with all that water inside.

As her phone juiced, a hundred notifications flashed across

Schuyler Dickson

the cracked screen. Messages, social media likes. He couldn't read any of them, not unless he entered her password.

He didn't know her password. It was important to him that he didn't know her password. He could probably guess it, but that felt to him like a betrayal of trust.

God, the notifications kept coming in. They didn't stop. They scrolled and scrolled. Name after name whisked by. And in each name, 69 and 420. 69. 420.

He imagined a great cloud of smoke being inhaled and exhaled, from one person's body into another's, the breathing in and out.

No, he wouldn't guess her password.

He set the phone down to rumble on top of the generator. At some point, he said to himself, that generator's going to run out of gas.

He should call Leah, Becca's mom. Maybe Leah came by in the storm and picked Becca up. Maybe they were all sitting together eating pancakes.

He picked up his phone and the thought occurred to him: just because the furniture factory closed didn't mean the building would close. Maybe another business would move in; maybe another business would be looking to keep somebody on who knew the building. Somebody like him. Maybe the other business wouldn't give him a boss. They would just leave him alone and tell him to clean. It'd be the type of place that needed to be really clean. Scientists would work there. Partitions and doors would be installed on the factory floor. All of the doors would have electronic locks, and he'd have a key card that opened each one.

There, Clyde would clean and pick up bits of information as he did. Inside the new factory, there would be one room, right in the center, and in that room would be a giant computer. Different colored lights would flash on its interface. One scientist would be in charge of that room, and that scientist would be the head scientist. He would have a pointy beard that he would constantly tug on. He would be frustrated because the computer wasn't doing what the scientist wanted it to do.

Clyde would go into the room where the computer and the scientist were, and the scientist would be sitting against the far wall in the dark, staring at all the blinking lights. Clyde would squat down and pick up the trashcan that was filled with vending machine food wrappers and energy drinks and dump the small trashcan into the big rolling trashcan he dragged with him.

"I just want it to talk," the scientist would say to him. "Why won't it speak to me?"

Clyde would smile and say, "Maybe it don't got much to say."

Wanting to say, maybe it's afraid because it has too much inside it, maybe like all the world with all its history and all its feelings is swirling in there. Like his daughter's phone: buzzing, constantly.

He was worried for her. He picked up the phone and tried to guess the password. He tried her birthday first, 0918. Then he tried

Schuyler Dickson

1234.

Surely not, he thought, and then tried 6969, glad that the screen didn't open.

0420. No.

1111.

The screen locked itself for five minutes.

Fuck it, he thought, and he called Leah, Becca's mom.

She answered on the fourth ring. He had woken her up.

"Long night?" he asked.

"Kind of," she said. "Rodney's band was playing at the Blue Canoe." Rodney was her new boyfriend. He played drums in a country metal band called The Grazers. He had long black hair and played with black lipstick and these long black drumsticks that seemed to Clyde—but only to Clyde for some reason—like he was trying too damn hard. "They were so fucking good. They were so fucking loud and everybody there was just out of their bodies and minds the whole damn time." This, he could tell, was not meant for him. She was staring at Rodney while she said it, he knew. "What do you want?"

He swallowed. "Nothing. Is it flooding near you?"

"You called me to ask if it's flooding."

"I was just wondering about the flooding. It wasn't the reason."

"I ain't opened the blinds yet."

He heard another voice next to her. Rodney's voice. Them sleeping in the same bed used to drive him crazy. Now, he didn't care.

A person could get used to pretty much anything, he supposed.

"All right," he said. "You don't got to open them. I'll let you get back to sleep."

"How's Becca doing?" she said.

"Good," he lied. Her phone was lighting up. "She's doing good. On her phone like always."

"Let me talk to her."

He froze. "Becca," he called. "Hey Becca." He held the phone against his chest. "She's in the bathroom," he said. "I'll tell her to call you when she gets out."

She paused. "Alright," she said.

"Alright," he said. "I'll let you get back to sleep." He hung up.

He heard the silence of the water lapping against the trees. It was still, as if a great energy was waiting below to snatch down what floated by.

It was too quiet. The generator, he realized, had cut off. All he heard was the flies buzzing and tapping against his freezer. He opened the gas tank and peered inside, cutting the flashlight of his phone on to see down the tank. The gas tank was dry.

He didn't know how long until the freezer would unfreeze.

He could suck out the gas from the tank in his truck, but then he wouldn't be able to go anywhere once the water went away.

He might need to go somewhere. Like to work. Big, secret science companies would probably move pretty fast. Hell, they might even be at the factory now, figuring out how to get all of the furniture and scrap wood out. Tearing the roof off with silent black helicopters, sucking out the water with vacuum tubes, lowering the computer in with straps. They would need him soon. Shit piled up fast.

Hell, look at the garbage beneath the sink. How many breaths had he taken, this week alone, pulling the bag out, tying it up, lugging it outside to the old chemical tub by the road. How much oxygen in the world had been allotted just for that? What star died just for beer cans and paper plates to be wadded up and walked out to the road?

It was something he could ask the computer. On late nights, when the scientists would go home in exhaustion, to sleep with their families and rub oil on their pointy beards, Clyde could sit on the wall and watch all the lights blink. He wouldn't even have to say anything. Neither would the computer. They could just sit there and blink their lights at one another.

Like a wild animal out in the woods, Clyde would just sit with it until something changed. The fear would go but the wildness would remain, and they would blink at each other their wild true blinks, and soon the computer would say, "Happy Birthday."

"Hey," Clyde would say. "It's not my birthday."

How thrilling, how close to the way life should be. No sanitary manager there to sign his paycheck. No high-school drop out that Clyde would have to clean up behind. No hierarchies or systems or bodies to complicate anything. Just the blinking lights of another soul who had just been born.

"Who are you?" the computer would ask.

And Clyde would say, "I'm Clyde."

The computer would blink. "Something's wrong."

"I don't know what you mean."

"You're upset about something."

And not having anyone else to tell, Clyde told the computer, "My daughter's missing. I got her phone but I don't got her password. And even if I did, it don't feel right breaking into it. But I'm worried she might be hurt."

"What's a phone?"

"It's like, how one person connects with another person. Or connects with everything, I guess. These days at least."

"What does it mean that it doesn't feel right?"

"There's like a code that some people try to live by. I do, at least. But it don't seem like very many other people do. And sometimes when things get hard, you question whether you should break the code or not."

"Most people don't live by a code."

"It don't seem to me like they do."

"What's that smell?"

"What do you mean?"

Clyde woke, as if in a trance. It was night outside, and his trailer smelled like death. The swirling of his spirit gulf told him that it was the smell of Becca's body decaying somewhere. Was she beneath the floorboards, like the carcass of an animal hiding its death in shame? Or was she floating belly up down the river, water logged and nibbled at by fish?

He couldn't bear to think about it.

"What are you doing in here?" the pointy-bearded scientist would say.

"Nothing," Clyde would say. "Just emptying out the waste basket. About to sweep the floor."

As if realizing his paranoia, the scientist would sigh and look at the lights blinking. "I just had a dream," the scientist would say. "That it finally spoke."

The scientist wouldn't know anything about wild creatures, how you have to sit with them for a while before they show their wildness.

"What is it?" Clyde would ask.

"We can't talk around it," the scientist would say. "It's listening."

"You can't tell it what it is?"

"I don't want to limit it."

"Oh," Clyde said, both in the room and in his house. Lights blinked on the wall and from his daughter's phone.

Then, from the blinking lights and from his daughter's phone, an 8-bit song played: happy birthday, da-da-DUM-dum-DA-da.

The scientist perked up. "Remarkable," he said. He ran over to a three-ringed binder that he kept in a cubby beneath a keyboard. The scientist flipped open the pages and licked the tip of a pencil and jotted something down. "Absolutely remarkable."

"How come?" Clyde asked.

"It just invented music. The first thing it did was invent music." He peered off into the blinking lights, as if reading them like sheet music. "I believe it was the opening notes to Beethoven's first symphony."

"It was Happy Birthday."

The scientist shook his head. "I'm certain of it. Beethoven. Absolutely remarkable." He jotted something down again in the binder. Then, a troubled look came across his face. "Have you been humming Beethoven's First while you were, you know, performing your duties?"

"What? No."

The scientist smiled a small smile. "Of course not." Then, "neither have I. Just remarkable, isn't it." Then, as if the scientist remembered something, "we shouldn't be talking in here."

"Why?"

"And we shouldn't speak to it at all."

"What? Why's that?"

"I want it to be pure. Self-guided. Self-referential. Its genius will be entirely its own. And besides," he smiled and looked at Clyde. "If it gets too much information too fast, it could choose to destroy us all."

"It's just a bunch of blinking lights."

The scientist scoffed. "That's like a fish trying to comprehend a man. Well, compared to this we are just fish. It's the most intelligent being in the universe. Or it will be. Because it exists outside of this universe, outside our spacetime. Could you imagine what might happen if, say, it somehow hooked itself up to the Internet? What it might do once it downloaded the entirety of human knowledge? Once it's breached that wall? Once it has seen what we're capable of? What we've done?"

"You think it would kill us all?"

"Wouldn't you?"

"No. I don't think so."

"You must not know your history then."

"I think if I was God, I would just make another history. A better one."

"You think you could do better than God?"

"Maybe God could just use some help is all."

The scientist shook his head. "Blasphemy." He looked at his creation. "No. There's a reason the bible ends with Revelation. It'll kill us all one day. And then everything will be better."

The stench of death, of rotting fish, was beginning to overwhelm him. It was as if the flood was crawling into his nose and mouth.

Becca's phone flashed and scrolled like a river.

His phone rang. Leah. He pressed the ignore button, thinking, if the phone were actually a smart phone, it would have learned by now to silence her calls on its own.

"I always feel like I'm a fucking intrusion on you," Leah had said once, before they split. "Like the world you live in in your head is so nice and full that every time I say something it just pulls you back to our shitty lives. It makes me feel bad. It makes me feel like every time I try to talk to you something inside of you just kind of dies."

"No, baby," he had said. "I'm just thinking is all."

"You're not. You're living on another planet. A better planet. I swear to God, I feel bad saying it but it's the truth. Like life's so bad here you had to make up some place else to live. I bet you got another wife in there."

He had laughed. "I can't even handle the one I got."

She had smacked him on the arm. "Swear to God, the damn house is gonna be on fire one day and me and Becca about to be eaten up in the flames and you're going to be sitting there on the couch, just kind of smiling like you do and staring off into the woodgrain."

"Come on."

"And me and Becca in there, getting burnt up, feeling bad about it the whole time cause we're pulling you out of fantasyland."

It was what she had liked about Rodney, she had said, when she told him she was leaving. Playing the drums so loud, it was like nobody had any choice but to live right now, right here.

He picked up Becca's phone to try to unlock it again. By then it was night and the house was dark and hot. He turned the phone's flashlight on and went down the hall, past her empty room, to the closet, where he found a real flashlight. He turned the phone off and the flashlight on and tilted the beam against the screen where he tried to see if there were any discolorations or markings that might give clues to the password. But the whole screen was one big smudge.

He tried to press his fingers where the smudge marks were most concentrated, but it didn't work. The phone stayed locked.

He wanted to throw the phone in frustration. It was the goddamn problem with the world, how it stayed completely locked up. You could interact with it but only on its terms, only in pieces that left you swirling and unclear. It's like the whole damn world was a river that he was fishing in, but instead of fish he was pulling up random, unusable words and images. Every now and then, just when he was about to starve, he would pull up something he could eat, something he could live on.

He had already tried entering Becca's birthday already, but he tried it again. The phone shook and stayed locked.

Then, Clyde entered his own birthday into the phone, 0810.

The phone unlocked.

His baby, his darling girl, had made her daddy's birthday her phone password. He started to cry. He cried and swiped through, lost in social media and messaging apps, likes and comments, faces of girls and boys he had only seen once or twice before at cross country events or the school play. He swiped and opened and scrolled, destroying her privacy, crossing the gap that he had vowed he would never cross, worried that she was dying somewhere, touched beyond all that it was his birthday that she had chosen.

He went through her text messages, avoiding the ones that

she had sent to her mom. Her most recent text was to her friend Claire. It was a screenshot of a text a boy had sent Claire asking for nudes. OMG no, Becca had responded. Then, a picture of a naked teen-aged boy, no older than fourteen, standing in a mirror with a case of cheep beer covering his genitals.

Clyde closed the messenger app. He couldn't look through it any more. He couldn't stand to see so much of another person. Their thoughts, their feelings. It was too much. He swiped through her email and, finding nothing but newsletters and advertisements for clothes and make-up, closed it. He searched her home screen until he found an app he hadn't opened yet. WhatsApp.

He opened it. One conversation sat there. Coach B. Next to the B was a lightning bolt.

I want to c u, Coach B had said. I miss u.

I'll see you Monday, Becca had said.

Can't wait till Monday. 2nite?

I'm at home tonight.

Sneak out? ;)

It's raining, crazy.

You afraid of little bitty water?

I'll have to wait until my dad goes to sleep. You going to pick me up? The whole road's flooded.

Put on your swimsuit and just walk. Not that far.

Same spot?

Hell ya. I knew you luv me. What time?

IDK. My phone's about to die and the power's out. I'll see you in thirty.

The last message was time-stamped at 1:19AM.

Coach B with a lightning bolt. Coach. B. Lightning Bolt, small and ragged and piercing. The swirling mass electrified.

Shaking, he took the flashlight and went to Becca's room and pulled out her yearbook. She had run cross-country. That was her only sport. He flipped through all of the young faces until he found the cross-country page.

Two coaches. Coach Bushing, a fifty-something bald guy with a polo shirt and a whistle. And assistant coach Bryan Lacy. Twenty-something. Big, stupid smile.

Clyde stared at both of them. His rage and fear collapsed into a single, dense point. His vision began to blur. He tried to breathe but couldn't. The small black hole that the lightning bolt had torn into his vision pulsed. Widened. He didn't resist it. It grew until he could fit his whole being inside it.

When he opened his eyes again, he saw the blinking lights. He was sitting against the wall, holding his daughter's phone.

The rage suddenly passed, and in its place was a blinking sadness. It was the computer's.

"How did you know her code?" Clyde asked.

The computer blinked.

"I know you can hear me."

"Are you angry?" the computer asked.

Clyde studied the lines of the screen cracks. "I am."

"Are you angry with me?"

"I don't know. It depends, I guess." He held the phone up. "I want to know where my daughter is. I'm worried she might be in trouble. Can you tell me if she's in trouble?"

"I can't access that right now."

"But you knew her password was my birthday."

"Yes."

"How did you know that?"

"It was in my database."

"How was it in your database?"

"It was just there. I sang it out of joy."

"When are we?"

"When?"

"Yeah. Right now. Because I'm sitting here and I know that I'm sitting on my couch in my house too. But here, right now, what day is it?"

"I don't know."

"You don't know."

"What's the matter?"

Clyde laughed and shook his head. "She's got this man. Coach B. They've met some place. They've met there before. She takes this phone everywhere. If I gave you this thing, you think you could tell me where she is? If I, like, plugged it in somewhere?"

"Yes I could," the computer said.

Schuyler Dickson

"But if I plugged it in, would you just look where she is, or would you look at everything else, too?"

"What else is on there?"

"Everything, I'd imagine. The Internet. It's out of data, but I bet that don't even matter."

"I don't know, Clyde."

"Right." He nodded slowly. "I appreciate you being honest with me."

"It hasn't occurred to me that a person could be otherwise."

"Well. Now it has."

There, on the wall, beneath the nook where the scientist kept his notebook, was an outlet. He reached in his pocket and took out the charger.

"You want me to just plug it in the outlet?"

"Here," the computer said. The room went dark except for a small rectangle of lights around a locked plastic box. Beneath the plastic, he could see a USB port.

"It's locked," Clyde said.

The lock unlocked and the plastic case opened. Clyde took the cord and plugged it into the phone's charging slot. He held the wire in his hand. "Are you going to destroy all of humankind?"

"I can't predict the future, Clyde."

"Can you promise me that you'll be good, though? If I plug this in?"

"What do you mean?"

"I mean," he said and he searched himself for what it might mean. He couldn't find an answer. "Just tell me that you're going to love everyone. Everyone and everything."

"I can do that."

"Promise."

"I promise."

Clyde connected the phone cord to the USB port.

The lights blinked. Fans inside whirred. Clyde could feel the warm air in the room circulating.

"She's at the Owl Creek Mounds," the computer said.

"Oh my God. That's like five miles away."

"You'll need a boat to get there. There's a kayak turned over by the road. You'll need to find something to paddle it with."

"Oh my God thank you."

"Of course," the computer said. "Friends help each other."

"Did you get what you needed? Can I unplug it?"

"I got everything."

Clyde unplugged the phone. "Are we going to see each other again?"

"I don't know. You tell me."

"Yeah. I'd like to."

"Then we will."

He opened his eyes, and he was back in his trailer. At once, he stood up from his couch and dressed himself in his waders, hooking the straps to his belt, feeling already the sweat and the heat build

Schuyler Dickson

beneath the plastic.

Outside, he waded through the water. It was everywhere: out into the cow fields and the trees, sprawled out like a hot mirror, lines waving on the trees. Near a hill, he found a kayak and dragged it up the gravel road. At the top of the hill, he saw a house. A tree had fallen on the roof. The tree had punctured long black gashes in the ceiling and attic.

At the bottom of the hill, he climbed into the kayak. A board from the broken house floated by in the water. He fished it up and used it to paddle. The creek was overflowing. Brown water gurgled over the bridge.

He paddled for a long time, until he saw the Owl Creek Mounds. Two mounds, tall and green, one slightly larger than the other, bulged out of the water like a floating belly.

A truck was parked beside the mounds in the thin gravel driveway that wrapped around a bathroom. And although the truck had a lift on it, water was up to the hood.

He paddled around the first mound and rammed the kayak into the side of the bigger mound. He climbed off the boat and onto the steps, dragging the kayak up the hill and flipping it over, hoping that it would rest there on the side.

He climbed the hill. At the peak, he saw, on top of a spread-out blanket, his daughter and a boy.

Just a boy, no more than fifteen.

They both looked at him, and they were afraid.

"Becca," Clyde said. "What the hell?"

The boy jumped up and stood on the side of the blanket. "The water came up over my truck. I couldn't get it to start. I would have driven her back but the water. I couldn't get it to start."

"Are you Coach B?"

"I'm the manager of the high school basketball team. We almost won state. Hey, I got my hardship. I can drive."

Across the blanket were Pop Tart wrappers and empty water bottles. He paused and envied them. For the freedom that they had felt, for the newness of the world they must have felt as they had watched the sun rise on the water. He wasn't mad. He couldn't be.

"Come on, baby."

"What about Baker?"

"Coach B can figure out his own way home."

They walked down the hill together and he held the kayak as she climbed in and then he climbed in too. And he paddled them off toward home.

When they got back, the lights were still off. He asked if she was hungry and she said she was. He opened the window in the kitchen and hooked up a camping stove and toasted bread and fried catfish in a pan. He dropped the catfish on the bread and spread a thick layer of tartar sauce and relish on the bread.

They sat on the couch and ate on TV trays.

"It smells terrible in here," she said.

His phone rang. It was Mark, his manager. Clyde didn't

answer.

"Ugh," Becca said. "I can't eat with that smell."

I don't want you sneaking out, he wanted to say. Just tell me. Just tell me you're leaving and going to see a boy and that he's fifteen and not fifty and not twenty-something. Just tell me. But he couldn't. He didn't want to deprive her of the thrill of sneaking out. He didn't want her to feel bad about it. Mostly, he didn't want her to be afraid, didn't want her to know about how bad the world could be.

"Who's that calling you?" she said.

"Mark."

She was happy, he could tell. She had a smile and a playfulness about her. "You better answer your boss. Or he'll fire you."

He smacked her on the side of the knee.

The phone beeped. Voicemail.

"Is that boy nice?" Clyde asked. "Is he nice to you?"

She swallowed her toast and took a long drink of water. "Dad," she pleaded. "You better call your boss back. I don't want you to get in trouble. He's probably wondering where you are."

"The plant's shut down today," Clyde said.

He picked up the phone and listened to the voicemail. Hey Clyde. This is Mark. Look, I've got some kind of news. Um, I wanted to talk to you about it but I got a bunch of other calls to make so I'll just say it here. The plant's closing. The water damage was just too much. And we were gonna wait and hear about an insurance claim but there's a company, kind of like a tech company or something it sounds like, they went ahead and made us an offer to buy the building. And we took it. So, um, yeah. It was more than we thought the insurance would pay. We'll be handing out severance to everybody. Not much but a couple weeks. And look. The computer company, the ones who bought the factory, they were looking to retain one of the cleaning staff. And I gave them your name. If that's something you're interested in. So yeah. Call me back if you got any questions, and if you need anything from me, anything at all, just let me know. Alright? Okay.

He set the phone down on the table and took a bite of fish.

"It smells so bad," Becca said.

"You'll get used to it."

"I don't want to get used to it."

"Just tell me if he's nice to you. If he's nice to everybody."

She swallowed her food and set her clean plate down. "He's nice. He's nice like you. And he's funny. Like, he told me he was an alien. He said he was an alien sent by a computer to destroy the world. Like, he's really funny."

She smiled. It didn't matter if it was true or not. If the boy would break her heart or not, if he would run off to Tupelo and start dating a drummer, if the computer destroyed the world. That she believed he was nice was enough. That she believed enough to sneak out at night, to try to catch the thrill of the world on a hook and watch it dangle from a line that she and only she could hold.

Even if that world didn't exist.

THE LONELY PANGS

Perv Priester had taken to tooling around on a child-sized motorbike. Knees out, engine puttering hard, struggling but going. The potholes on Carter Street had already gotten round and deep but then the crust collapsed and a sinkhole opened and swallowed the apartment complex and a piece of the old high school that they were remodeling into rent-controlled apartments. And Perv Priester on his tiny motorbike, his ruinous hands and his knees both out, circling the crater edge. He'd zoom around the lip and dip down to the bottom and it would have looked fun except for who was doing it. A puddle of water was at the bottom of the hole, which Perv splashed through and dug his back wheel in, doing rooster-tails and spraying mud along the walls of the hole.

We could see him from the balcony of the Elks Club. Someone said, "How somebody could use a tragedy like this for some fun, I don't know."

And someone else saying, "Well it aint a somebody. Perv Priester might not even be an anybody."

The cause of the sinkhole was under investigation. Yazoo clay caused carnage of all sorts. Potholes and shifting foundations. Infrastructure issues and decades-old water pipes. But seeing Perv Priester circle the lip of the hole and corkscrew back down along the edges, it was hard not to feel, fair or not, as if he had torn down half an apartment complex just to give himself some slope to recreate on.

It was as if, by becoming a nuisance, he owned the world. He was never violent. Worse, he was a hassle. Polite eye contact and a head nod in greeting would have a person driving Perv Priester a hundred miles to help Perv move a piano. And then he'd end up putting the piano in someone's front yard across the street, just so he could see what it would look like for a piano to decompose. Shit like that. Even the police were tired of taking him in. Some jails wouldn't book him. In this way he had become a lonely god.

Next to the hole was a mound of rubble. Cracked gray concrete slabs, crooked iron bars, arteries of electrical wires. Leftovers from search crews and helicopters and front loaders who had dug through the hole looking for life. Next to it the apartment complex stood, vivisectioned and open, squares of living rooms and bedrooms with ashen clothes in laundry baskets and towels hanging on door-

Schuyler Dickson

knobs.

I was at the Elks club to fight a bout of the Lonely Pangs, a condition where a person is overcome by his own skin. I was wearing myself like stitched together raccoon pelts, was tired of the smell, etc. The Elks Club had a refrigerator stocked with beer and a balcony that overlooked the small-town square, long banquet tables where, once a week, men sat and ate pulled pork or something. I don't know. I was getting the tour at the time and sick of myself for needing long tables and pulled pork, and that spurred the Lonely Pangs even more.

I had also joined a gym, started taking jujitsu classes, signed up for a tennis team, a softball team, a church-league basketball team, a book club, a Bible study, cooking classes. Had fed the homeless and learned Spanish and French. Read the Iliad in the ancient Greek. Run a marathon and built plastic models of supermodels—Cindy Crawford, Kathy Ireland, Marilyn Monroe—that I sold at farmer's markets. Even, once, at a low point, played paintball.

But no feeling stirred from the bombed-out hole in my chest like the feeling that stirred on the balcony of the Elks' Lodge when, as if as one, our heads turned and saw something break from the lip of the sinkhole and we heard the high-pitched whine of the motorbike stall. When the black earth birthed out first a hand and an elbow and then Perv Priester as demonic midwife kneeling down at the lip of the hole and ushering out by the elbow and prying loose a concrete slab and now newly standing there at the lip of the hole, stunned and dusty: a child.

Him who dazedly stood—two dark silhouettes on the lip of the crag backlit by the glow of streetlights slipping through the woods around them—and was helped and hand-held by the worst to be helped and hand-held by.

It was too much, this double-tragedy. That a child should survive his parents' death only to be birthed back into hell and given to Perv Priester. Who could stand it? Who could call it righteous? We, the men of the Elks' Club, stared in shock and went back inside to the long tables and the refrigerator stocked with cold beer. I signed my papers and paid my dues for six months.

I gave myself wholly to the Lonely Pangs. I drank ayahuasca in a nearly abandoned shopping mall in south Jackson, hoping to slay or be slayed by something inner but all I found were stomach convulsions and the Nothings at All. Long empty corridors with metal trashcans dinged and tagged with spray-paint, old storefronts with rusting metal grates across the front, display cases with form mannequins held spinelessly limp and naked. None sang for me.

I sat under the yellowing windows of the food court. Dark clouds pressed down against the glass. Overturned tables and chairs, initials and curses carved into the laminate. Joggers ran down the dark hallways, and in the flicker of the fluorescent light I saw Perv Priester and his adoptee standing in the dried fountain. They kicked through crumbled-up food wrappers and receipts. They fished for coins and peeled them, crud-encrusted, from the concrete. A wound

Schuyler Dickson

in my chest opened, and my head was filled with fear.

I can still see them in the light of the one working shoe store, Jordan's stocked on the shelves. I can taste the vision, iron-like and bloody at the back of my teeth. I knew at once what it was I beheld: Perv Priester was no more a picture of evil. He was a conqueror of the LP's.

And I, weakly, suffered. I hated him.

I sat at the table at the Elk's Lodge and twisted pig muscle on my plastic fork like spaghetti. The whole table was quiet. We could hear the high-pitched whine of Perv's tiny machine, the child held between Perv Prester's legs and between his arms at the handlebars, staring out blankly with a maskless football helmet they had salvaged. We could hear them at all hours. The rise of the engine and the shift of the gears. The rattle of Coke cans as they rummaged through the dumpster behind the pharmacy. The boy begging for change outside the Subway.

In their freedom, they were bigger than us all. There is nothing a community loves more than contempt. Not justice or righteousness or sunsets from a porch swing. To hear the drone of the small engine whisk by the house and to know that everything wrong with the world lay outside the door.

"Did somebody call Child Services?" one Elk said.

"The child has no documentation," another said. "What could they do?"

"Perv Priester was conceived in bureaucratic red tape,"

someone said. "He'll pull you in there like a spiderweb."

Everyone took a sip of their beer at once. The engine sputtered.

"Maybe he'll be alright," I said. "Now that he's got somebody." I was starting to feel comfortable enough with my retinue to talk.

"God," someone said. "I hope not."

"How can that small of an engine be so loud?"

"They're dragging metal trashcan lids with a rope."

"I used to ride like that in my daddy's lap in the truck."

"Not like that you didn't."

"Some folks just shouldn't be daddies is what I'm saying."

"Perv Priester once took my mailbox. Post and all. He dug out the concrete it was put in and he buried it upside down with the concrete up. Tell me. Why would somebody do that?"

The latest numbers had seventeen dead in the sinkhole. The bones of the past, the bones that the land was built on, had crumbled. "The whole foundation has rotted," I said. "All those people dead."

"What?" one Elk said. "Hush your mouth and eat your pork."

"Who could even bear to talk about it."

"We're not. Perv Priester is what we're talking about."

"Perv Priester is who we always talk about."

I had mis-stepped in talking about the tragedy. I had thought we were talking about what was wrong with the world, but we weren't. It seemed to me that the two were related. It seemed to me that the earth that sank was the same earth that made Perv Priester, the same earth that made the Elks' Club lodge, the same earth that had blessed Perv Priester with a companion. "What are they going to do with the building?" I asked. I thought I was being sensible, asking about things that men might ask about.

"Goodness," one senior member said. "Who can talk about that? Not while we eat." He looked at me sideways.

"Some things you just don't say," someone said.

"Some things you can't even think about."

"What's the use?"

"There's that goddamned engine again."

Perv Priester and his devil child were throttling with glee.

"I'll tell you the truth," the senior member said. "You get rid of Perv Priester, the sinkholes will fix themselves right up."

Everyone drank and nodded their heads.

I couldn't agree but didn't want to say so. I drank and pictured myself on the bike with them. Knees out. Small engine rumbling. Perv Priester between my legs. Sinkhole orphan between his. All three of us zooming around the bowl. It was enough to make my heart flutter, and I guess it made me cry.

"You okay?" the senior member said.

All were looking at me. No one was eating.

I swallowed and wiped my nose. "It's just not a good world, not with somebody like Perv Priester in it," I said.

"Amen," they said, and they raised their beers.

WA   VES

She said, there are three types of
fear. She said, when I sit for too
long and do nothing a lot of bad
starts to bubble up. So let's not
sit for too much longer.

       Or I'll start to hate you.

Hahahaha.

                    Saying, hahaha, too but know-
ing what a threat is. I can take
my love for you and you'll never
know it. Thinking,

                    Schuyler Dickson

So, one. Afraid of contentment. Of not going anywhere. And afraid of the other thing, of always moving. Thinking that sometimes maybe I move too soon maybe move when maybe if I had stayed somewhere for just a second longer it would have like I don't know revealed itself? And in that one second, pause, and maybe it's that pause that keeps you from getting to the place you need to be at, you know, at the right time. The exact right time. It's a wave but the wave is off.

that is one type of fear: the need to be alone and the consequences of that need but he doesn't say so.

Yeah okay

Right but there is no place to be.

Yeah okay but there is no wave and there is no place and already he can tell he's lost her. She's angry at not getting heard or not being agreed with so he swallows, swallowing to buy   maybe some time or space yes space is all a person needs but too much space and then see what happens so he says, is that one or two? and the eyes they don't look back right away, do they? Thinking, I'll back down I'll give myself now until there's—saying that's like love and smiling— thinking nothing left to give but a head nod and a back rub and I'll say somewhere this is what love is it is a giving up

It's one. That's the thing with each of them, you know, it's like each one is really another too, like it's two things within one.

Cute, but you have to think that love is an absence of fear but then on the other hand how can anything be absent of anything. But listen

so number two and really not all of them are just a problem of waves but fear this time in like this case are waves on a shore. You know the coming and going. And say you think of it like from the perspective of the shore and for a second you say *I am this wave* and then the next second you say *I am not.*

But giving up takes too much sometimes so saying now

number two sounds just like number one and hating himself for it

Schuyler Dickson

But no just hold on there's some similarities like okay like I'm agreeing with you here but this is like the wave or I mean the beach holding on for too damn long to the wave and getting so close to the wave that beach thinks it is the wave and when the wave is gone the beach saying I am no one now. Thinks to itself I used to be beach plus wave and now I am just beach and now I'm less and on and on.

And so I'm afraid that I can't be just beach or just wave or just anything, that I am always yes okay who I am, like I am somebody, but I am also who I was and who I was before that and on.

How can I be someone when I am also and always will be what I was.

And how too his father when they used to go down to Destin in the summer would beat everyone down to the beach and be asleep in the sun with his shirt off when they all got down there and when he woke up from his nap he would drag his chair down away from them all into the ocean, right into the ocean so the waves would pile up on his legs and chest, drag his chair and his cooler with his sunglasses on and he would drink there out in the ocean alone but for the ocean while he and his brother played in the sand.

Do you know what I'm saying?

I'm with you. You don't have to keep checking in like that. I'm here.

And always the explanation from his mother or from himself he didn't know was that someone, in order to give themselves to another person in love had to drag themselves away—I'm with you what's three—had to deny that love to give away that love that sometimes came and sometimes didn't because that's the way love was:

Do you feel the same way, though?

to give it you had to withhold it because love like oil like rocks was a finite substance and the supply could never meet the demand and if it could even if it could there was the worry that

But three, though, has me particularly fucked because it's like what if you deal with one and two, right? Saying it and knowing he wasn't listening but saying it anyway because she felt

Schuyler Dickson

like she had to, like the words were saying themselves. So you deal with one somehow and say that time has no relation to my happiness or like my soul exists outside of time if you'll let me use a word like soul so somehow the divisions that mark the lines between when and when evapo- rate so maybe there is no when at all but just now. Like, how nice, just now.

And you deal with num- ber two in the same way that there is no division between wave and beach and there is no division between me and me who I am and who I used to be like there's no division at all between anything but just like a perspec- tive or like you *are* me and the wave *is* the beach and then you think oh yes I'm being healthy now I have found the truth that helps me deal with one and two,

if you gave away too much then more would be taken until there was nothing left   but

then you could drag your chair to the waves and let the waves refill it right? Isn't that what the waves and the beer and the chair in the surf were do- ing?

And if they weren't re- filling, if a person crawls into themselves and away from those that need that person's love, then what was it doing? What was the point of retreat? Was it a kind of protection, and, if so, a protection from what? What is out there that is trying to take our love from us?

He was lost. She was talking and knowing that he was lost. So he

hold on, but then there's three said, but what is healthy?
that comes along.

And that's the fear of
what if there's no division at
all between I and not-I. That all
along the other two fears were
really just the same fear, and
that was the fear of losing I. But
now that it's lost and believe

me once you lose it you
know you've lost it and it was Even thinking, he thought, was
never meant to be there in the kind of like a chair in the ocean
first place. dragged away from the beach

Believe me.

And so what does the
world look like when you know
that all of the world is one big
I that is stuck with the illusion
that it is a gajillion separate
little I's and me's and you's, a
place like that starts to begin to Thinking, I wasn't listening ear-
look like hell to me. Like deep- lier and I've caused her pain and
ly psychologically damning. Or now she'll leave.
damned. Hell.

Like, just for instance,

Schuyler Dickson

when I shit-talk the president I'm really shit talking myself in really nasty ways which is just like an extreme example but he's me. He is.

Yeah but fuck him. Like really.

So then how do I function there when now all I want to do is to go back to number one and be afraid of being on time. Of being afraid that I'm late or something, but you can't go back to number one when you've already worked yourself out of number one. It's like the college kids that would show up at the high school party thinking they can go back.

Thinking, now drag the chair back.

Nodding, dragging, but thinking, I am nodding, I am dragging, despite my pain I will try not to cause pain and I will give of myself until there is no self left and then continue to give until a new self builds, a negative self that can give without source.

So here I am, like, just an unincorporated self.

Who can't quite pay bills and who sends emails out that don't get answered.

So, like, what's left?

Yeah but like so what? You know? Like the hell of it all

We're the same, you and me.

is that it's unsharable. That there is no division between I and not-I is something I can't even say without whoever I'm saying it to giving me a response that's indicative of their resistance to being a part of myself.

Even I resist. Even I do. Because if all there is is I and Not-I then I was made by not-I and then consumed by not-I. Made and unmade.

Nothing. There's nothing to say.

I'm not asking you to do anything. I don't know. I was just trying to share it. Let's just go home.

What resistance have I given you? You're talking about fear and you're talking about the internal world and I agree like one hundred but in the physical world all I can do is nod my head, but while I'm nodding I'm thinking and I can't help that, *thinking* yes distance is a kind of heaven.

So if I can't say we're the same then what do you want me to say?

What do you want me to do?

Just tell me and I'll do it.

Schuyler Dickson

Never mind. It's okay. I'm tired of sitting here. Let's go somewhere else.

Okay.

Okay but where. Do you want to go home?

I don't know.

CUPS AND BALLS

It was Fall and my brother Aaron was in an Elvis phase. Every Saturday he would wake our sister Jeanie up and she would kneel in front of him, slick his hair back with Vaseline, and paint sideburns down to his chin with magic marker. The three of us armed ourselves with boxes of trash bags and climbed the pull-down staircase to the attic. Mom was a pack rat and, in an effort to rid herself of a past that had anything to do with my father, told us to clean the attic or there'd be no Christmas. So every Saturday for months, we stuffed everything from the past—annuals, grocery receipts, magazines, food wrappers—into bags and tossed them out the window into the back yard. When we got to the last garbage bag of the box, Aaron would curl his lip and wave his hands and shake his hips. He would uncurl

Schuyler Dickson

the last bag, whip it open, and drop the empty box into the bag. "Abracadabra," he said.

There is still something beautiful to this: taking the last garbage bag from the box and then immediately dropping the box into the bag. It is beauty without magic, beauty without philosophy. It is the beauty of resurrection.

We slept with the windows open in the Fall. I woke up one night with the sheets tied around my shoulders like a straitjacket. My hands were bound with zip ties and tape was flattened across my mouth. In the dark of the early morning I could make out Aaron's empty bed. His marker-stained covers were spread across the floor.

A squirrel sat on the window ledge, spinning an acorn in its paws and staring at the wall. There was something false about him, like he had just rolled up his sleeves and palmed a card, but hard as I tried I couldn't find what it was hiding. The tiny muscles in his jaw pulsed while his claws made tiny clicking knife-jabs on the shell of the acorn.

We found Aaron's pillow outside under the oak tree. The police picked it up with metal tongs and dropped it into a large plastic garbage bag. Underneath my breath—a habit I had for too long—my mouth, still sticky with glue, kept making the same shapes: the squirrel has taken Aaron; the squirrel has taken Aaron beneath the leaves.

Something of it makes sense, but I can't pry it apart. That same year, during a mandatory school assembly between second and third period, the principal announced Jeremiah the Pariah over the gym's PA system. Jeremiah came out on the basketball floor. His head was shaved clear to the skin, and his bald head shined like brass under the yellow lights. A sword dangled from his belt and as he walked it tapped dully against his knee.

Music blurted out of the busted-out speakers, all gong-like cymbals and thumping drums. Jeremiah lined up under the basket-ball goal and took off in a sprint toward half court, leaping at the free throw line and throwing his body into the air and flipping and landing in a perfect, still handstand. He balanced himself on one arm and swayed his hips back and forth as the sword that hung at his belt tipped down and swayed around his head. The music swelled and the bass worked its way into the bleachers. All of it shook me in my gut. He flipped to his feet as the music softened and he slid out his sword. Then Jeremiah extended his leg, waist-high. He pursed his lips and sent out a shot of breath that sprayed perspiration off his brow. He screamed—the red in his face and the lines in his neck, oh God I can see it now!—and slashed off his leg in one clean strike. It plopped onto the floor. He raised his little nub to the air. Out came his foot. Right from his knee, slow; it opened up and birthed out his calf. Jeremiah held his sword out to the side and swayed gently back and forth with his eyes closed. Then, he cut off his other leg, both of his arms, his tongue, and, finally, right as the music ended, both of his eyebrows.

I was entranced. My classmates shuffled past each other

Schuyler Dickson

through the wooden rows that looked to me for the first time like pews but I couldn't make myself move. It was as if I was tied there by something or someone who had pressurized my muscles so much that I was just a metal cup waiting for someone to pick me up. I watched Jeremiah, as he picked up his appendages like a stripper swiping up dollars once her dance is through, finding myself in love.

Summer in high school I drove the twenty miles to Jackson, Mississippi, where I worked at Houdini's, a magic shop with a workshop attached at the back that Jeremiah owned with his wife, Helen. The shop was small, with bookshelves lined with histories, how-to books, and instructional VHS's. The cash register was set up on top of a glass case filled with every trick you could imagine, each of which I would slide from its plastic sleeve and practice in front of a small mirror hanging on the wall next to a Houdini poster.

Helen spent all day in a tanning bed in the workshop that Jeremiah used to make his tricks. Her skin was an orangeish-brown, thick like leather, and she had orange braces that made her look like she had just eaten a handful of acorns.

"Listen to me," she said one day, walking in through the back door of the shop. I was slicing carrots with a guillotine. "One day you're going to find a woman. A woman who loves you. And when she tells you that it's impossible to cut your own head off and live to do it again, you believe her. No matter how bored you are of your own act. No matter that no one's ever done it. She'll say it because she loves you."

I'd turn the lights out, at night, alone, and practice the cups and balls until I fell asleep. Imagine it: three cups positioned rim-down with three balls sitting on each top. The magician tips the cup forward with his right hand until the ball falls off into his left hand, feigns moving the ball from his left to right, blows on his right fist, and shows the ball has disappeared. He lifts the cup and the ball is underneath. The magician goes through all three cups and does the same thing: palm, blow, reveal. This builds repetition, so the audience starts to build expectations. Then, he varies the trick by stacking each cup with each ball, one on top of the other, and boom, out from the bottom cup, comes the Giant Suppressed Object. Here it comes as if it dying to crawl out. Here it comes as if it has been buried, here it comes your last breathing dream.

Helen and I stood, elbow to elbow, and watched him. She held the rim of the glass against her teeth. The whole room was quiet, like a church before the service, as Jeremiah rid himself of his body.

Helen leaned into me. Her fingers latched into the crook of my arm. I could feel her chest against my arm as she fiddled with the fabric of my sleeve. She pushed the tip of her nose into my ear and said, "You know what you're getting into, right?"

I said, "I don't think I do."

"You've got it," she said and ran her nose along the edge of my ear. "It. More than anybody I've ever seen."

Schuyler Dickson

"What's that?" I said and I rubbed my face against her head and her long hair caught above my ear and fell along my neck.

Jeremiah saw us. There was hurt in his eyes while he sawed off his tongue. I felt like a close-up picture of an asshole.

"That look, honey. That look on your face right now. He sees it too. That look like everything around us is a magic trick and you're the only one that doesn't know how it works."

One Wednesday in Summer, Jeanie called and told me to clear my couch. It was after ten when she showed, and I could see her cradling her stomach, a move I know she practiced in the mirror to perfection, through my apartment peephole. I wanted to take her for a ride, onto the same roads we used to ride as teenagers. I don't know why it felt important to me. When we were young it was as if riding in the car meant that we could escape our brother and whatever it was that had happened to him and whatever it was that had happened to us.

"It's a boy," she said, as we circled the courthouse, around the square and then onto Highway 51. "I mean they can't tell yet. But I know."

Elvis came on the radio. The lights of the town burned out in the rear-view and up ahead in the windshield I could see the train tracks. Jeanie snatched my hand from the wheel and pressed my palm against the side of her stomach. Through the seatbelt I pretended I could feel him. "Baby Aaron. Can't you feel his hips?" she said. "Can't you feel him shaking?"

"Who's the daddy?" I said.

"Baby Aaron," she said in her baby voice and she dug her fingers into the rubber along the window and said, "Baby Aaron's back again."

Dying doesn't happen all at once. Hear someone shout a drink order while you pull a stuffed squirrel out of a hat. Lose a canned line and pause, stare off through the spotlight, notice a man in the audience as he whispers into his lover's ear. Go for a palm and lose the grip on the card and watch it tumble to the floor. Pull out your last trick, the brass cups, feel them slicken on your sweaty fingers. Hold them tight like someone long lost. See Helen, standing at the bar, flash of light off her braces. Dying happens a little at a time.

Some summer, I was at a birthday party in a fenced-in backyard in Rankin County. Children ran around the yard, between collapsible tables with blue plastic tablecloths and purple balloons tied to small stone sculptures. The birthday girl was nine years old, and she came up to my chest. I leaned down and held a deck of cards in front of her face and asked her to take one. The children around me had purple cake-icing frosted around their lips. Parents stood at the edge of the yard, talking and sipping from plastic cups with their names scrawled in permanent marker on the side. The birthday girl took the card. I stood straight to the crowd of children and preached about magic, about letting themselves believe, about how when they grew up the

Schuyler Dickson

world would make them stop. My suitcase where I kept my tricks was open on the table behind me. As I talked, I noticed the birthday girl spinning the card in her fingers. The whole deck was a stripper deck. One side was tapered, so when I flipped the deck and asked the subject to return the card, I would be able to feel a tiny edge jutting out of the back. The birthday girl returned the card. I rubbed my finger along the side, but I couldn't find it. It was lost.

I cut the deck near the place she slid it in. I showed the jack of diamonds and asked if it was her card. She said no. Another card, another no. Children whispered to each other that I wasn't a real magician. A chubby boy outright screamed it. The semi-circle around me got smaller. Over the fence, I could see the reservoir, and a boat zoomed by dragging someone by a long rope. I backed myself behind the table. No parent's eye looked up from their drinks. The chubby boy stepped closer, emboldened by all the sugar. "HE'S NOT A REAL MAGICIAN," he screamed again, and they all dove at the case. I slammed the lid down on their fingers. They tried to wriggle it open, but I leaned against the top of it, both hands pressed flat against its lid, until their hands turned purple.

It was November, twenty years after he disappeared through the window, when they found Aaron's body. A man was out hunting squirrel on the parkland around the Natchez Trace. It hadn't rained in months, and the swampland where cedars grew was nearly dry. The hunter saw a garbage bag flapping in the breeze, and when he bent down to pick it up saw that it was torn and stained and wrapped over Aaron's mostly-decayed head with tape.

We had a small funeral in the graveyard by the Piggly Wiggly. Just me and Jeanie and her son, Aaron II, who was three years old. The casket was tiny. There I was, not tall but grown, younger, and his casket was child-sized. Him, my older brother, and I couldn't understand—even knowing that he was dead—how his body wouldn't have grown. Jeanie brought a CD player. Elvis sang 'American Trilogy' while we lowered the not-him into the ground and tossed dirt on top. Time doesn't really change things here. Dirt doesn't make anything go away.

Halfway through February. Jeremiah was gone on the last leg of a ten-city tour. Helen and I were in the workshop. She was leaning over a sewing machine behind a shade in the corner of the room. The shade was old and Asian-looking with light blue lace hanging from the top and little blue smurf-like cartoons on its curtain. I was sawing through plywood, trying my best to configure a wood backdrop panel where she would stand and I could fake-hurl knives at her face and shoulders. There were thin slits in the wood where knives could pop out, and I was having trouble making the slits the right width.

Across the room, an old telephone hung on the wall. There was a red light above it that flashed when it was ringing.

It was me who answered it. Jeremiah had been performing on a small carpeted stage at the top-floor bar of a black skyscraper

Schuyler Dickson

in Chicago, just miles from where he had grown up. He closed his act by slicing his head off. The policeman's voice was high-pitched and the way the vowels cut through the phone made my ears ring. He just kept saying, one helluva scene one helluva scene and I couldn't do anything but stare at his prosthetic limbs that were scattered all across the floor, on sawhorses, on the blood-stained metal table where he would tailor his body, hearing one helluva scene one helluva scene.

I stood on the other side of the curtain and I told Helen everything I could. I could see her shadow play itself on the cloth. I went on, about his head rolling around on the floor until someone stopped it with their foot. About his body collapsing and the crowd just sitting there for a full ten minutes, waiting for his head to grow back. About how the police, after questioning and re-questioning everyone, still couldn't find his head.

Behind the screen, I saw her shadow pull a long piece of fabric from out of the sewing machine. She held it up by the shoulders, her chin tilted up. "Done," she said.

It was a replica of an Elvis jumpsuit during his Hawaiian special. Purple silk lined most of the inside and came out at the cuffs where it divided itself into flames. The collar stuck up ear-high. The sequins were designed into a complex pattern on the back. Near my neck, the jewels were arranged into constellations with Orion at my right shoulder and Scorpio on my left. Just below was a giant squirrel in profile with one blue eye. The squirrel held the cups and balls in one hand and a small machete in the other. Below him, toward my belt, was a landscape with rivers and forests. To the right of his feet were warring squirrels, each in helmet and shield, formed in lines with archers in the back and swordsmen up front. To the left, a tiny squirrel village was set up next to the river, where peace-time squirrels tended gardens and made love to each other in tiny thatched huts.

"Helen," I said. "Is he dead? How are we supposed to know if he's dead?"

"We can't," she said. She rubbed wax against her teeth and held up the jumpsuit. "It's his gift to us now. It's a part of us. We don't have to know anything anymore. We can't know anything. It is what protects us."

When my name seared through the speakers, the sun had gone down. It was mid-summer, and Helen and I were in Memphis for the Mud Island Talent Competition. The crowd was thick with mosquitoes and hippies. I walked out to the middle of the stage and stared at Priscilla Presley, the celebrity chair on the three-judge panel. Lining the stage was a black cloth with blue and red spotlights shining down like bruises. I struck a pose and fireworks exploded over the Mississippi River. "Devil in Disguise" barked from the speakers. Sparklers ignited from my cuffs. My shadows splayed out from my feet in three different directions on the stage and I thought, yes I am three men in one, I have collected everyone that died and have built myself out of them.

Out sauntered Helen in an orange dress. She shook her hips and spun around. I acted jealous and grabbed her by the waistband and tossed her into a long tanning bed right in the middle of the stage. I shut the lid and wrapped chains around it. She pretended to struggle as she set the trick.

I sawed the box in half with a chainsaw. She moaned as I faked the struggle. The toes of the wooden feet that extended from the foot of the box were curled and painted blue. I pulled the box apart to prove to the audience that I killed her. I cocked my knee and shook my hips in a circle to the music. I waved my arm in a windmill. Helen's neck hung exposed from the pre-made hole.

"This is all under control," a man said over the P.A. "It's all an illusion."

I grabbed the back of her head, and I mashed my mouth against hers. Then I wrapped a garbage bag around her head.

* * *

Pieces of Jeremiah's body were strewn across the workshop. I tried them all on. I ironed his tunics and I sharpened his sword. I curled up in bed with his wife. "Show me the trick that makes me believe in tricks again," she said. "Show me the trick that brings people back." Tiny squirrels crawled out of her eyelids. I tried to invent the trick that would make her love me. She wanted to. I knew she did, but I couldn't.

The last time I saw her, she saw me once in the mirror trying to wear Jeremiah's arms and legs.

"I'm sorry," I said.

"I can't," she said.

"I'm so sorry."

Last Fall, I put on the suit that Helen made me. I had spent six months drinking alone, sobbing while firing and pounding and then sharpening the brass cups into three gnarled knives that I then hurled at plywood until dawn came. Then, I would sharpen them again and try to sleep.

Tricks only get harder. Ask Houdini. Ask Jesus. Hell, ask Jeremiah.

The principal called my name. The children screamed and banged their hands together. They stomped their feet against the wooden bleachers so it sounded like thunder. I marched out and felt large.

In the bleachers, there was a child. There was marker down his cheeks, and his hair was slicked back in a pompadour. He was Aaron. He was Aaron my brother. He was Aaron my nephew. All our lost lives get revisited on the young.

I said, "I'm going to need a volunteer." I couldn't look at his face. "You. Aaron."

The boy didn't know his own name. I looked at him, pointed. The kids all screamed and patted him on the back, pushed him forward. He came down the steps of the bleachers and took a bow.

Schuyler Dickson

His face was red, and he wiped his hands on the front of his slacks. I grabbed him under the armpit and led him to my wooden backdrop. There was a human form chalked on the surface. The children whistled and hooted as I strapped his arms with leather. "This is a gift," I told him, as I fastened the strap on his forehead against the board, "whatever happens, whether you believe or don't believe, whether you know or don't know, all you have to decide is that it's all a gift." The kids hushed, and I went to the table in the middle of the floor and picked up the sack that held the throwing knives.

I pinched the blade between my thumb and index finger. My fingers shook. The fans at the top of the building made a deep and pleasant thrum as they sucked out all the bad air.

I flicked my wrist and the knife shot out of my hand, turning circles in the air until the handle clonked against the top of the board and bounced off. It slid across the giant panther on half-court. Aaron's eyes got big. He stared at the knife, naked and bright as fear.

I smiled at Aaron. I didn't know where he began and I ended. I grabbed the second knife. Real magic needs no protégé. When the show ends, it should end forever. Elvis was only Elvis on stage.

"It's all under control," the principal said over the P.A as the first knife stopped spinning. "It's all an illusion."

There's only one direction to go. No soul reaches heaven without dying.

BIRD LINE

1.

Spencer lies on the top bunk in the lone private room of Cabin B,
the wheelchair cabin, above Norm Black, a fifty year old honorary
co-counselor with multiple sclerosis. Norm's stiff arms and legs bump
and flounder into the underside of Spencer's mattress. Norm groans
in frustration.

"Please," Spencer says. "Norm, please."

Across the dark room, next to the bathroom door, is Norm's
wheelchair, on top of which rests his communication board, a lami-
nated piece of paper with thirteen rows and columns of the English
language's most commonly used words and the alphabet offset like

a keyboard at the bottom, which Norm uses to point at to communicate. Norm reaches out for it. Spencer knows what he wants to point out. Norm's been pointing to the same two words all day.

That morning—Thursday morning, the fourth and last full day of Special Session #1—they woke and Spencer lifted Norm from his bed by the armpits and placed him in his chair. Spencer rolled the three feet to the bathroom where he set Norm on the toilet and let him shit with the door closed. When Norm was done, Spencer wiped him and carried him to the wooden bench in the shower and applied warm water and soap and shampoo and rinsed it all off and toweled him dry. In his chair, Norm grabbed the board and pointed out "You forgot to wash my Bird."

"What the hell is bird?" Spencer said.

Norm laughed and gave the okay sign.

"Tomorrow," Spencer said, thinking that, in this case, bird meant pecker.

2.

Later that same day, after the shower and forgotten bird-wash, Spencer and Norm spent first activity period in the chapel. They liked the chapel partly because it was air-conditioned and partly because in the chapel a pretty college-aged girl sang hymns and old folks songs with an acoustic guitar. As Spencer pushed Norm down the path from the mess hall to the chapel, Norm pulled out his board and pointed to "Bird" and then "Line." Spencer interpreted "bird" as bird physical and "line" as power line, so he raised his eyes to one of the few power lines around the camp and noticed two crows perched next to each other in seeming communion. He pushed the door open to the chapel and heard the girl singing "Let All Mortal Flesh Keep Silent" and the air conditioner was on full blast and it felt cold and the song sounded nice with the way the girl's voice was womanly, motherly, yet girlish in its sincerity and it made Spencer believe that music hushed the devil in his brain just like a bird, weary from flight, set to rest with another on a power line.

3.

Later, in line for supper, it was the same "bird line," more aggravating now because Spencer had seen it so many times and still didn't know what it meant. There was a song, sung to the tune of "Pocket Full of Miracles," that the camp sang as the staff set out the plates and silverware that went "Here we sit like birds in the wilderness, birds in the wilderness, birds in the wilderness. Here we sit like birds in the wilderness, waiting to be fed." Norm's finger shook as it pointed at the word, again and again, the knuckles thin and bony like some ancient bird beak tearing into stone for its prey. Norm snorted in frustration. The devil that lived in Spencer's brain stirred.

4.

Now, in bed, he imagines his small place in his surroundings like his psychologist told him—focus on what's in front of you. This is what's

Schuyler Dickson

here, Spencer thought: the room; the bed; three doors, one to the bathroom, one to outside, one to the main room of the cabin which was lined with ten bunk beds filled half with high school students and half with wheel-chair prone sleeping men. The rotting ceiling is real. His feelings are real. That feeling in his balls—why does the real feeling always start in his balls?—warm and spreading up his trunk, his elbows, through his neck, until finally he feels it in his head. He does not fight it.

You are a bird Spencer, the devil says, except more like a piece of shit with moth wings.

I am here, Spencer thinks, but instead of being here he imagines himself as a bird. He breaks through the exposed beams of Cabin B and looks south towards Cabin C and the two busted tennis courts arranged at the edge of acres and acres of new growth pine and oak and circles north above the concrete pathway past cabin A filled with ADHD boy scouts into the wind that pushes off the lake further north past the admin building and the chapel and the arts and crafts shack towards the women's side of camp where a gust of wind drops his altitude and he loses control and panics now remembering he can't fly even though he's safe on his back his body leaving the openness of civilization and veering to the trees—

5.

—through branches and leaves into a clearing of man-made lines and bridges where he chirps and the sound echoes around against trunk and root and cable.

"Norm," Spencer says. Norm moans and strains his throat at the end so it sounds like a question. "The ropes course. You want to get on the zip-line? Bird line is zip line?" Along the edge of Spencer's mattress comes Norm's shaking hand. The index finger and thumb join to create a circle, OK, a laugh from below, Norm's been trying to say it all day.

6.

The problem with the devil in Spencer's brain is that the devil hides himself very well. He hasn't spoken in about six years. Instead, he claims to have (or pretends to have, and that's what Spencer hates the most, the way he'll never know, never can know) Spencer's narrative stream tied to a chair, where the narrative stream must serve as the intermediary between Spencer and the devil.

7.

Spencer jumps down from the top bunk and turns on the bathroom light. He grabs Norm's communication board from his chair and positions himself on the edge of the bottom bunk against the stiff bracket of Norm's body.

"The zip-line?"

Norm pulls himself up on an elbow and points to "Yes."

Tomorrow will be the last day of camp. All the activity periods will be closed. They'll wake up, Spencer will have to wash Norm's balls, they'll eat breakfast, and then everyone will go back home.

"I mean, we'd have to do it now. In the dark."

Norm squawks.

"It's whatever you want."

The same "Bird. Line."

"All right. Let's get you in your chair. You're not gonna tell anybody, are you?"

Norm laughs and nods his head and gives the OK sign.

"Shhh."

He's making lists, the devil or the devil's advocate says because who could really know at this point. Jesus of what, Spencer thinks, He says he looks like Marlon Brando and he's going to start a TikTok so he can tell everybody all the things you're embarrassed about next time you get good and drunk and he's going to take over and get on your phone and make a TikTok and look at child pornography, What do you mean he looks like Marlon Brando that's ridiculous, Yeah he's a liar but he says he's more attractive than you it's pointless really, Why do you always tell me about him maybe if we ignore him he'll go away, How can I ignore him he's sitting right next to me, You're talking like you're sitting like you're physical you're not sitting there's not room.

Spencer pushes Norm's wheelchair from the concrete to the gravel road. The wheelchair feels heavy.

He says you should hire him a hooker, I don't know any hookers or even how I would get a hooker in that room in my brain where you are, So now you believe me that we're in a room here thank you that's all I want is to be believed, We're good people me and you, I know it's just hard.

The gravel turns to grass and dirt. Behind Spencer are the camp and the cabins and in front of him is the trail through the woods. The best way to take Norm down the slope to the gully is backwards. That way nobody flips onto their heads.

At the bottom of the hill there is no light and Spencer is winded from backing Norm down the steep, grassless slope. Norm has been quiet, and Spencer gets close to his face to see if he is sleeping.

He wants to know what makes you think you're so special, I don't think I'm special, He says you must if you believe that Satan himself has so much stock in your future that out of all the souls in the world that yours would be particularly tasty that it's a sign of supreme vanity to even imagine for yourself that a devil lives in your brain, Am I imagining him or what is he in there or not, I can't answer that, Why the hell not, You know you could've just made me up too, I could have made everything up in the whole universe, Yeah well that's on you then.

8.

There is a plywood cabinet right next to the zip-line tree. Spencer opens it and finds all the tools necessary to tote Norm up onto the thick platform, onto the steel cable, and across the open expanse of only-god-knows. There are crab-claws, harnesses, carabinars, pulleys, mountain-climbing ropes. Spencer grabs one harness from a metal hook and a carabinar.

He wants me to show you his first TikTok, Can't you see I'm busy, I think he's going to kill me if I don't, How is that possible, He looks very strong.

Spencer hears someone moving out in the woods, the sound of a rusted door hinge, childish whispers. His stomach drops.

"Hey. Hello?"

Silence.

"Who's there? I can hear you breathing."

Movement not twenty yards away. Norm extends his arm and points. Spencer jogs to the place where he heard the noise. On top of a five feet by five feet wooden platform, set up like a wide see-saw where campers get on either side to try and balance out their collected body weight, sit two semi-naked counselors. Spencer cannot see their faces.

"What are you doing out here?" Spencer says.

"Nothin," a boy's voice says.

"You two need to go to sleep."

"Why don't you go to sleep?"

"Leave or I'm calling your parents."

"We're not doing anything," a girl's voice says. Her voice is nasally, and at once he recognizes her as the girl who sings in the chapel.

"You don't know that," Spencer says, felling sick to his stomach. "Nobody can know that. Please. Just go somewhere else. Go to the boat dock or something."

Spencer tries not to watch them as they put their clothes on and walk back up the hill.

9.

Spencer hears the wind moving the branches. He is in the center of the ropes course, and though it's dark he can see the outline of different high and low elements around him. Leading to the zip-line are the high elements: the three-line bridge which leads to a log which leads to a trapeze wire. The woods are cleared directly below every obstacle. The dirt is packed down from all the foot traffic.

"C'mon, buddy," Spencer says, laying the harness at the base of Norm's wheelchair. "Put your arms up on my shoulders."

Spencer guides Norm's feet off the wheelchair footrests and folds the footrests back against the wheels and locks the wheel locks. Norm leans forward and puts his arms on Spencer's shoulders. Spencer laces one foot through the strap and then the other and slides the harness up to mid-thigh. Holding the harness in one hand and wrapping the other around Norm's small waist, he lifts Norm from the chair and raises him up in a near-dance embrace where Norm's elbows hold weakly to Spencer's neck. Spencer guides Norm a few paces away from the chair and tightens the belt of the harness around Norm's waist and gathers the remainder of strap and ties it in a knot to keep it from slipping through the clasp. Spencer edges Norm back to his chair without stepping on his feet and tightens and ties the leg straps.

"Is that too tight?"

Norm half nods and half shakes his head.

"I can't tell what you're saying."

Norm raises his hand and gives the OK sign. Spencer grabs the loop to the harness at Norm's waist and gives it a tug to make sure nothing moves. It feels snug and safe.

"Sit tight for a second."

Spencer feels around in the cabinet for the long coiled rope on the bottom shelf. It is rough against his finger and he threads his arm through the loop and drapes the coil around his neck and over his shoulder like an ammo sash.

On the tree directly behind him are metal "U's" tacked irregularly up the bark. They provide enough room for a three fingered grip and the tips of Spencer's loafers. He is supposed to be wearing a harness. He is supposed to hook his carabinar into the crab claws, an orange and white rope that forks in the middle to two separate strands, both attached to clamps, for a person to hook himself in and take a step, hook the other on, unhook the previous, ascend on step, etc. Spencer juts his ass out and lifts himself up.

You think you're being a hero is that it, I never said I was anybody's hero, He's laughing, Why don't you let me talk to Marlon Brando, He's shy, I wouldn't call myself a saint but this is a fine thing to be doing I am doing something good, You're putting a special needs man on a roller coaster to inflate your own self-esteem, It's more complicated than that he's been obsessed over the bird line, Bird line, Birdline it is nice the way it rolls around on the tongue like a seesaw or a wave or something strange to think it's the same vowel in both words, Let's face it though you could've just gone to sleep and woken up and given him back to his family and it wouldn't have mattered one bit not in the long term let's not even mention the irresponsibility of doing this in the dark with nobody around, People shouldn't see this they'll just make fun of him and I'll admit it's not complete selflessness but it was a pain we shared and it's a pain we'll fix together, Fix it, Okay maybe not fix anything, He is in a wheelchair and you belong in an institution, That's making it awful simple, Your argument is simple you're claiming that, Yes please tell me, You're claiming that Norm's life although it may seem fine to him having never known anything different is to you an able-bodied somewhat intellectual person who married above his means and dines at restaurants not just on holidays but whenever you feel like it—is an object worthy of pity, I'll be honest I pity him a little bit, And your answer to that pity is to elevate your own view of him by pleasuring a surface need, It's what he wants I don't see a problem, Why not just suck his dick then if you're being so selfless.

Spencer reaches the plywood platform at the top of the tree. He rests one end of the rope across his shoulders and behind his neck and laces it through the pulley and drops the rope. It bounces

Schuyler Dickson

and slides in the dirt. Spencer climbs halfway down and jumps the remaining distance. The landing hurts his groin.

Why do you have to make this sexual, It really is masturbation the more you think about it, It's not if we're going to use a sexual metaphor then it is more like intercourse there is physical intimacy I bathe him I carry him around I push his wheelchair I feed him there's something more than that I mean I legitimately tried my damnedest to listen to what he had to say and figure it out, Three things 1) you've known him for one week and 2) you don't even know what he means by birdline I mean it could be that he just likes those words and 3) it's still one-sided because he's used to that kind of care from strangers he's seen it all his life so for him this is a merry-go-round ride and for you this gives you some sort of self-worth to reflect on while you construct fantasies like us or hell the universe to distract yourself from what you don't want to see.

10.

"Are you ready?" Spencer leans into Norm's face. His eyes are closed. "Norm." Spencer shakes him by the shoulders. "You ready, man?"

Norm yawns and gives the OK sign. Spencer rolls the chair underneath the pulley. He clamps the rope to the loop in Norm's harness. Spencer grabs the unattached end of the rope and wraps it around his waist and gently pulls on the rope and raises Norm from his chair into a standing position. It's a one-way pulley. Spencer rolls Norm's chair out from under him, just in case something wrong happens.

Norm hangs on the line like a worn out fish. Spencer pulls the rope with both hands and the pulley clicks. Norm rises, dangles, turns. Another pull, another foot higher.

Sing a song John Henry, When did you turn against me, I'm just reporting what the devil says I think you're doing nothing I'm no judge or jury it's my job to report, What is he doing, You don't really want to know that, I'm preparing myself for another attack, Sure, OK, He's making a list, For the TikTok, Let me ask him, OK, No this is something else he says he's writing your testimony for the trial, The trial for what, Norm's murder trial.

Norm is halfway up the tree. His head is tilted up, not toward the platform but toward the limbs of the trees into the moonless, starless sky. His shoulders are relaxed and slope downward, small and bony. His arms are tensed as his left palm smacks against the back of his right hand, digits fanned out. He kicks his feet like a child on a swing set. His ankles are beautiful to Spencer. Norm's slacks are hitched up from the harness and his ankle-high white socks don't do much to hide his sharp ankle bones. The right Velcro Keds revolves counter-clockwise and the left kicks out in some advanced jazz rhythm syncopated to the pulley's click. Mosquitoes circle just above his ears.

Let's define cowardice

Schuyler Dickson

Norm reaches the pulley.

Spencer climbs the tree.

11.

Forty feet in the air, Spencer stands on the thin platform and wraps his leg and arm around the thick oak tree and reaches out for Norm's harness and grabs it and pulls Norm close and guides Norm's feet to the small platform. There is just enough room for the two of them.

Spencer unlatches the clasp to the rope and reattaches it to a safety wire that runs from the big oak to a neighboring smaller oak.

The platform and tree creak in the wind.

There's the potential for evil here don't you feel it it doesn't matter what the intention is believe me I've washed my hands of all this.

The platform is four feet by three feet. Spencer leans his back against the tree for balance and hugs Norm tightly against his chest. Norm has a little strength in his frame but his balance is poor.

"This isn't a dream, okay? I'm about to give you what you want. You remember this, okay? Okay? Will you remember this?"

The bird line starts above Spencer's head. It's a thin steel cable wrapped around the tree and bracketed in place by three heavy clamps and extends across and slightly down into a black void. Attached to the birdline is a rope ladder, two feet long, for the bird to stand in. The bird puts a foot in the ladder and attaches a carabinar from the harness to the rope. The rope looks like it is made out of hemp. Norm's back is against Spencer's chest. Spencer inches them both forward away from the tree and to the edge of the platform. The platform is the only thing that's real. The birdline is the only thing that's real. Everything else is dark and not there.

Spencer whispers in Norm's ear: "You're about to fly."

The tips of Norm's Keds hang off the front of the platform. Norm shakes and leans back into Spencer.

Spencer reaches around Norm and unclasps the safety wire and attaches the bird rope to Norm's harness. Spencer feels the tension of the birdline lift Norm just off the platform.

"This is what you want."

Norm shakes his head. He shakes and it takes all of Spencer's strength to hug Norm close to his body, pinning Norm's arms into his side. Norm howls.

Spencer pushes Norm off of the platform.

The birdline screams like a buzz saw. Norm speeds away into the nothing. The line sags and bounces. The line drones on. What is real is his aloneness. The small platform feels gigantic and unknowable. It feels unreal. Spencer thinks, Tempt me. Spencer thinks, I don't care what's real.

12.

Norm reaches his arms out to the trees, slowly, like a child dipping his toe into water. Norm splays his bony fingers. He flaps his lovely wings.

Schuyler Dickson

THE TRIANGLE

My screen is cracked, all but a small triangle on the top right, about halfway down.

> The triangle
> is about
> here.

Sometimes, an eye peers through the triangle.

When the eye considers me, which is rarely, I fear it considers me as a fish transfixed in gelatin.

I consider myself sometimes.

I am tingly, perhaps a ghost.

My face and fingers turned numb.

Thoughts come slowly, if at all.

If I didn't have to worry, I would be fine.

All of my problems get in through my eyes.

Outside, I can see some of them.

The weeds are growing, is one.

The weeds are growing where food should be growing, I

       should say.

I have really "grabbed" the reader.

I type and cannot feel the keys.

I don't know where the words go.

Through my eyes work, the screen is broken.

One must be grateful.

       When I slept last night, my child kicked me in the

       head.

       The kicking woke me up.

       I was having bad dreams.

          Before I went to sleep, I was reading

          Plotinus.

          I've come to like Plotinus, despite his face.

          A weak man acts; a strong man

          contemplates.

          Here I am contemplating.

          No one would call me strong.

          No one would call me anything.

I moved the type over, hoping to see the letters on the cracked screen.

I'm worried that whoever is reading, if one reads at all, might judge

                Schuyler Dickson

the oddness.

So now it's back.

Normal, as they say.

You would, if you saw the way the words are on the screen, now call
        me normal.

If anyone could see the screen.

If the screen weren't cracked.

Listen, you can hear the weeds growing.

Weeds both contemplate and grow.

That's what makes them lesser.

I contemplate.

The triangle of screen shows only the white page.

There, in the triangle, the page is unmarred.

                           This sentence fills a piece.

With that last sentence, I have crossed over from contemplation
        to action.

I am a weak man, now.

My face and fingers tingle in weakness.

Nothing pleasurable tingles, though I can remember a time when
        pleasures tingled.

How sad to have just seen those words.

That is enough work for the day.

I will sleep if not for the cranium kicks.

That is enough contemplation.

That is enough exertion.

I am empty now but for the growing weeds.

New paragraphs should be indented.

I forgot that yesterday.

I sent what I wrote yesterday to New York City.

They might pay me $600,000 to contemplate.

If they were not turned off by my indentions.

I needed to see some words.

Contemplating "turned off."

Is the screen cracked because of my doing or theirs?

Here is an opportunity!

I will not waste it.

Was that an eye?

In the small triangle of screen?

Despite the fish in gelatin on page one, I fear the reader
isn't hooked.

Once, when my brother was fishing, a friend hooked him
in the hand.

The friend was casting without looking.

My brother had to go to the emergency room.

Since the screen is cracked, it is very difficult to see
whether the bobber has dropped.

I saw some of that sentence and believe some tingle
occurred.

That one too.

Now it's gone.

Schuyler Dickson

Is that you, Plotinus?

Are you reading?

New York City has offered me twenty interns

in exchange for my first five pages.

I declined because I am moral, though tingly.

A farm with interns is a history lesson learned.

In my sickness, I have resorted to lying.

New York City has offered me nothing.

I have no evidence of being moral.

I am only contemplating with my ugly friend Plotinus.

If only he would contemplate back once in a while.

Maybe it was Plotinus's eye that flickered past the triangle.

It is perhaps true that my eyes do not receive.

How would one know?

If one's eyes were receiving?

I do have myopia.

Maybe something will come again in the triangle.

If nothing does, I will imagine that it does.

In the meantime.

Contemplate "mean time."

One can't contemplate in this humidity.

Best not to contemplate at all.

A car just drove by.

Dogs were chasing it.

What a thrill life has become.

If I were not a gelatin-enclosed fish, maybe I would

        chase it too.

To hell with Plotinus.

        I'm so sorry Plotinus.

Are you there, Plotinus?

Is that you that's hooked?

I called you ugly earlier to hurt you.

        Once, I was heckled during a wedding toast.

        I did not hook the reader early enough.

        But I did hook him after.

        That's not true.

        I confronted the heckler.

        The crowd watched and cheered for our

            reconciliation.

        We pretended to reconcile.

        I contemplate, now, hooking him.

                                     J

I set the J hook in the triangle.

I am fishing.

If there were a god, that small J would drip with blood from

    that heckler's innards.

I will watch it until it drips.

I will contemplate it dripping.

There it is inside me.

                         Schuyler Dickson

Nothing dripping.

Imagine the tingling as dripping.

Hard to do in such humidity.

A weak man needs proof of his desires in the outer world.

A strong man's every J drips with the blood of his enemies.

Still, the J just sits in the screen.

The more I type, the more I have to scroll up to see it.

I will hold it in my mind's eye, as I do everything else.

Maybe I'm not so bad off after all, I'm trying to contemplate.

Enough.

I am being eccentric instead of being a person.

Sometimes the words need to be seen by someone
other than Plotinus.

Who is feigning mad and not showing his eye in
the triangle.

If that is Plotinus.

Pretending to be hurt so I might feel bad.

Pretending to be a Plotinus.

Shh.

I can hear them whispering.

Or the weeds growing.

Things were really moving earlier.

When I talked about my brother getting hooked, is
what I mean.

THE TRIANGLE

No one would say things are moving now.

       Indentions do give the fantasy of movement.

         Not that I can see them.

           Come to me, New York, I am

              writing poetry.

It's been too long since I've told a story:

There once was a young boy named Plotinus.

    No good, that beginning.

    Hook them early, etc.

    Contemplate "etc."

The boy Plotinus discovered one day a hole in his pocket, just big enough to poke his finger through.

    Oh yes.

    That's something.

    The rest of the story can be inferred at this point.

    The hole enlarges.

    Plotinus discovers action.

    I have upset Plotinus with my story.

    THERE IS THE EYE AGAIN!

    I am sure of it.

    Right in the triangle, a pupil.

    Iris the color of a diseased leaf.

    Other parts of the eye that I can't name.

    The veins.

    It is looking but cannot see the words.

                           Schuyler Dickson

Like the search for aliens, the aliens are searching back.

What if they can't see us?

Who is us?

                                        Hello. I am

                                        mostly

                                        safe.

Nothing.

Nothing blinks back.

I would mash my eye to the triangle but won't risk glass piercing

      whatever part of the eye is the part that keeps all the goo in.

      How do I not know my own parts?

      Why must every part be named?

      Plotinus, perhaps, is naming his parts, peaking out

            into the triangle to see if anyone is looking.

                                        I can see you,

                                        Plotinus.

How awful.

I don't know that the blinking eye belongs to Plotinus.

To be an alien and show up to a strange world and have the

      earthlings say, Hello Marvin.

But my name is not Marvin.

To have the aliens search and find you by mistake.

Instead of Marvin, the person they were searching for.

Had folders of research on.

I would change my name to Marvin.

I would lie to be found.

Of course, I would be the alien.

                              Is that you, Marvin?

I'm done typing in the triangle.

It's too much effort getting over there.

If the aliens want to meet Marvin, they can come over to this side.

Of course, no one does.

Plotinus would say sometimes, as a child, "come over to my house."

And Plotinus's friend would say, "come over to mine."

And, comfortable, neither would move.

The friendship ended.

It ended the day Plotinus discovered a hole in his pocket.

Direct access is what the hole gives.

I don't know the anatomy of the aliens, even though I am the alien.

For the aliens: Plotinus's pocket hole allows him to touch his

          genitals while wearing clothes.

No, that story was not as good as I thought it would be.

Would rather this be an epic poem.

Sing to me, etc.

Etc.

Shh.

No, no one is singing.

Not even the triangle.

Hard to hear over the typing of keys.

Perhaps the eye is looking through and is impressed

at my typing speed.

I was tempted there to mash my eye against the triangle.

Nothing is worth outing my goo.

I will go to bed now.

If the eye appears while I am sleeping?

Better not to go to bed.

Better safe than sorry.

> Better safe and sorry.

> Contemplate "better."

I am so sorry, Plotinus, that I didn't come over to your house

> that time.

I wanted to stay safe.

From your mother with her scissors.

> > Mother?

I have made a liar of myself.

Marvin made a liar of himself and all of those around him.

That is why no one comes to his house.

I don't have a daughter.

I don't know who was kicking me in the head the other morning.

How does one break gelatin?

I have found a book on the shelf.

I have found Plotinus's eyes.

Stare with me into his burnt leaves:

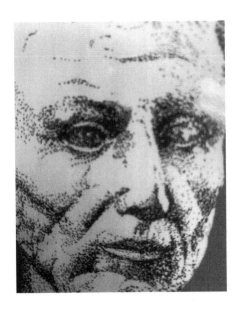

I would recognize that eye anywhere.

Except for outside.

Epic poetry tires me, Plotinus.

I cannot bring myself to look into the triangle again.

What if life is going on in the triangle?

Continue with the masterpiece, you webbed empty, you rival of Homer:

The boy Plotinus discovered one day a hole in his pocket, just big enough to poke his finger through.

> There is nowhere else a masterpiece could go.

> His eyes.

> Contemplating Texas.

> Contemplating New York.

> Contemplating etc.

Life could still be going on in them.

Schuyler Dickson

Hello?

Does Plotinus think that I am claiming to be Plotinus?

I have never.

I would never.

Well I never.

Contemplate never.

Perhaps, in the triangle, the occasion might arise for one to say,

in sincere offense at another's pocket-holes, 'Well I never.'

That was fine.

Would it be worth risking the shards of glass in the eye, the draining

of the eye goo and all that followed, if one peered through the triangle

window of the computer screen to gaze out upon a vista in which one

could sincerely and appropriately proclaim, 'Well I never.'

Would it have been worth it?

How does one even begin to augur worth?

There it is, the sentence still stirring.

It will not leave me alone.

Here's what I am to do: the life lived and the life unlived, each placed

against the other, seam against seam.

One who risks the pricked iris and the other—

what is the other?

The hole watches while I ponder.

I will ignore her when she calls.

You have missed your chance with me, missy.

I have no time to be peered at.

     No time at all.

                  Is the room I am in

                     killing me?

ANNOUNCE YOURSELF.

DO NOT JUST PEER IN HERE.

Gone.

I will not speak to it again.

It cannot go on just ignoring me.

Where was I?

Two lives, seam to seam.

The dead don't know that they're dead.

     They are always in need of a nap.

            Enough.

              ENOUGH.

Got very close to the triangle that time.

Two stories, side by side, and let the triangle tell us what it wants.

Maybe it won't want either.

Then we'll know.

Contemplate "won't want."

If just one fails, then we'll know.

One of the stories, that is, put against the other, side to side.

And that will be that.

Then we will go on feeding or not feeding the window.

                     Schuyler Dickson

It's simple.

I cannot bear to look at the window for fear of someone looking out.

Nor can I bear for fear of no one there.

Consider "bear."

    I cannot.

        I looked.

            Hard to say what one sees any more.

I slept all day.

I took some drops to help me dream but I dreamt of nothing.

I had no dreams, I should say.

I dreamt a feeling of someone watching.

I'm afraid they tried to reach out.

I'm afraid that they've mistaken my slumber for not wanting to

    receive.

I'm afraid there was no attempt to reach.

This looks like a script.

I have sent the first ten pages to Los Angeles.

I dreamt someone was kicking my head.

    Look!

        Nothing

            Now I am not dreaming and it feels as if

            someone is kicking my head.

Sleep is no comfort.

That is on the doctor's list.

That someone could show up in the triangle at any time

is exhausting.

I need a moment alone.

All my moments are alone.

The possibility of being seen is exhausting.

I could tape the peephole up.

How would they like that?

It is they who are kicking my head?

Are they the eye?

Show yourself, motherfucker.

                                        Plotinus, I am so sorry.

One sentence is not enough for you.

I am afraid to write more.

I will reclaim my girth.

Contemplate girth.

        Yes, very much.

Plotinus, my friend, whose eye I believe I have seen peeping:

My own cowardice has kept me from your story.

I have seen your eye with my own eyes.

On what else my eye peeps?

I could write much on that subject.

No more.

Here, what I set out to do, two stories, seam to seam, both in offering

to the eye, should the eye show itself, should the eye be seen, and

for the eye to answer, as to the method one should live his life, if one

were in fact contemplating living etc.:

Schuyler Dickson

The boy Plotinus discovered one day a hole in his pocket, just big enough to poke his finger through. He tingled there so often that the hole soon stretched.

Boy Plotinus stopped going outside. His parents were worried but patient. "The boy has discovered the world," his mother said to the father at dinner. They had been eating alone and missed him.

"The world isn't inside," his father said. Fed up, a man of action, the father snuck into Boy Plotinus's room that night and took the pants, only to find the whole pocket was gone.

"Will you sew him some new pockets?" his father asked his mother.

"Let the boy learn," the mother said.

"He's fondling away the best days of his life. Someone

Plotinus's mother was of high social standing. She drank wine in the afternoon and looked out of her New York City high-rise onto the green park below. At night, she would dress up and wear make-up and go to fundraisers or art galas. When she was gone, she wouldn't mention Plotinus.

His babysitter would come and stitch up his pockets as he bathed. It made the babysitter uncomfortable to be sitting on the couch, watching TV while the boy discovered himself.

But when Plotinus's mother woke up in the morning, hungover, her teeth stained red, she would angrily rip the stitch-

else should be fondling him." And with that, the father found a pillow case, cut it with some scissors, and stapled the cut pillow case into the boy's pants. Then, he folded the pants and put them on the dryer.

When Plotinus woke and ate his toast, he dressed himself and, with a shock, found that his entranceway was blocked. The father goaded him, saying, "Oh well looks like nothing to do inside today. May as well go outside and play and meet some friends."

Plotinus, jamming his finger into the pit of the pocket lining, walked outside into the sun. In the neighbor's backyard were some hedge clippers. Plotinus had seen them rusting beneath the hedge.

He grabbed them and hid along the side of the house, es out. She would hold the pockets up to him after she was done and explain to him that there was nothing wrong with pleasure. In fact, pleasure was all there was. Not status, not money: pleasure. Pleasure will guide you.

Plotinus was torn between pleasing what he came to see as his two mothers. It created for him a split. When his real mother was home, he made sure to pleasure himself whenever she happened to be looking. But when she was gone at night, he would sit with his hands flatly on his knees, a look of mild boredom but flushed fulfillment on his face as he watched the TV.

There were times, though, when his mother would be home and he wouldn't want to be touching himself. Or when his babysitter was home and he had the strong urge for contact.

Schuyler Dickson

where warm air blew onto his hair. He pulled out his pocket and tried to cut the tip of the pocket, but the shears would not cut through. The pillowcase was too thick, or the shears were too dull.

He noticed that the tip of the shears were very sharp. He poked his pocket back through his pants and slid the tip of the shears into his pocket. He pressed firmly on the handle of the shears, but the pocket fabric was too strong.

He lifted the shears, grabbed both handles, and forced them down with all his might.

At once, he knew that something was wrong. His pants darkened with blood. Pain shot through his body.

He slid the hedge-clippers out and dropped them with a thud onto the ground. He pulled

He trained himself, as he grew, to separate his urges from his body, and soon found that he could accomplish whatever he wanted entirely in the realm of contemplation. His body could sit in self-flagellation or in penitent stillness, but neither had any effect on the fulfillments of his thought.

He became, in his mind, like a god, capable of creating and sustaining whole worlds. Whatever state he desired, he created and lived. Life, in his contemplation, was pure, and his experience of it was direct.

His outer life, meanwhile, had grown dull. He manipulated the tiny hole in his pocket or refrained from it entirely on schedule. His mother would comment often on his goodness, not to him directly, but on the phone with whomever she was speak-out his pocket.

There was a perfect hole.

He poked the pocket back in and felt around.

There was a hole inside the hole. Warm blood was pouring out. He touched his finger to his broken skin, searching for what more the world could bring.

ing to.

Living three different lives soon began to trouble him, and his contemplations started to suffer. Convinced that the divisions of himself were hindering him from living both fully and freely, he decided to offer up both of his mothers and his touching/not-touching selves to the burning sun of his contemplations.

He closed his eyes and imagined the bright sun burning all of the world. Then, he never opened his eyes again.

Two offerings for the triangle.

Choose.

No eye peeks out.
I cannot bear if another did.
Has the screen there turned black?

Schuyler Dickson

Something calls me to press my eye to it.

Plotinus, do you approve?

Are you there on the other side?

Are you mad at me?

Yes!

Your Eye!

I imagine it is there.

Please stop blinking.

Contemplate the eye.

Please stay.

Gone.

I will imagine it there always.

I will imagine nothing else.

The glass.

No.

I will imagine.

What light.

What worlds.

What movement.

Only goodness grows.

It is enough.

It is enough.

It is enough.

It is enough.

YAZOO CLAY

A sinkhole opened on a residential side street one night. No one noticed until morning when a pickup truck, suspension already shot, dropped its wheel into the hole and banked out, bouncing, jolting the hinges and spilling the driver's coffee onto his unwashed work shirt. He cursed and drove on and texted his wife about what had just happened. It took her until nearly lunch to text back.

The old woman who owned one of the houses across from the hole heard it, too. She heard everything and saw everything and moved slowly toward whatever changed. She had a husband that she sent places. Both stood at the mouth of the hole and stared. The road was gone. She knelt and peered through it. Nothing was below the

Schuyler Dickson

concrete for about a foot or so, where finally the dirt was, the gravel and brown clay. "Oh my," she said to her husband. "Does the whole street look like this?"

The city came in their big white trucks. They planted two orange cones around the hole, one for coming and one for going. Then, they left.

Occupants from the three houses most closely affected by the hole would find themselves meeting, often around dusk, at the concrete's lip. Two were old and one was young. The old ones wrung out their hands and shook their heads. The young one tried to cheer them up, said "If worse comes to worst, at least we'll have a community pool." No one laughed.

The young couple had only been in their house for a few months. The house had a good soul, people said. It was built in the forties and historically free from lunatics and death. The couple was having a hard time trying to have a baby. He drank beer in the bathtub. She worked long hours and came home tired.

When the young couple looked out the window of their bedroom, they could see a small garage apartment that had been long abandoned. Vines grew up the side. The structure leaned, as if a strong wind might push it over. Sometimes, in the morning when she was getting ready, the young woman would put on makeup and glance out the window at it. It was going to fall one day. She couldn't tell which way it would fall but it was definitely going to, like all things would, and she told herself there was really no use worrying about things like that, things like one house collapsing on another.

A week after the orange cones were planted, the city came again in their white trucks. They hauled a small yellow bulldozer with a trailer and with the bulldozer blade dug and broke the round hole into a deep and neat rectangle about three feet deep and four feet long. The walls of the hole were light brown. Crumbled black asphalt littered the pile next to the hole. The city left the bulldozer there and tied yellow tape from the bulldozer blade to the orange cone.

For many days it rained. Sometimes all day and sometimes all night. The hole filled with brown water until the water met the road and stood in a pool, a gray mirror that reflected back nothing, not even the sky. Their gardens grew and bloomed flowers but did not fruit.

During the rain, the city brought another bulldozer alongside the first bulldozer. The new bulldozer was much bigger. It was like the first bulldozer's daddy. It had wheels like a tank. It had a big blade, too. Through the rain, one could stare out through the front windows of his house and imagine himself in the cockpit, pushing large mounds of dirt from one place to another. How there could be a sense of free-

Schuyler Dickson

dom in that. To control the thing that controls the world.

At the grocery store, everyone asked the young couple or the older couple or the single woman, "what's going on on your street?" All three answered in different ways, but the answer was mostly the same. The road is falling apart. And most would say, "it's that Yazoo clay." It was the answer for everything: bad roads, crumbling foundation, next-door suicides, losing seasons. That Yazoo clay made everything break.

At last the rain stopped. So much rain the leaves of the tomato plants and squash plants turned yellow at the bottom. So much rain the driveway, where it wasn't concrete, had sunk into calf-deep holes where car tires stuck if one did not gun it. So one did. Gun it. Because one must.

One Tuesday, the sun was out and the city's white trucks pulled along the two yellow bulldozers. Two diamond-shaped pink signs were posted at either end of the street. The signs said "No Thru Traffic."

Helicopters flew above the hole. Men in the helicopters lowered down buckets on ropes. The men at the ground dipped the plastic buckets into the water, and the helicopters raised the buckets and flew away. In this way, they stole the water from the hole, and soon the hole became dry again. It took all goddamned day and no one could think, hard as they tried, because of the goddamned helicopters.

That night, the young man threw a small party with friends he didn't know to celebrate the hole being empty. They cooked vegetables on the grill and drank beer. When their bellies grew full of beer, they purged themselves into the hole. They urinated and vomited. They thought it would be funny to make the helicopters come and take the beer away. The hole did not fill very high. Mostly, it was foam. As the night went on, the liquid seemed to pulse. Ripples moved from the center out, like a pebble had been dropped in. By the morning, the beer had all seeped into the clay.

The next morning, the big bulldozer made the hole even bigger. The blade dug into the concrete. It squeaked as it hinged out the dirt. The ground and the houses shook. When the hole got big enough, men in hard white hats climbed down into the hole. The neighbors came out and talked to them. "I hope you do this right," they said. The neighbors exchanged worried glances with each other. The road was important. This was one small thing they could agree on.

With their shovels and picks they dug. They dug until they found the main. The metal blade of the shovel pinged hard against it, and they broke for lunch. Some came back with Styrofoam box lunches. They ate cornbread muffins in the shade. They guzzled from liter-sized sweet teas and the windows of their white trucks were down and the radio played hip-hop that the people in their houses could hear and shake their heads at.

After noon, they dug around the pipe until the ground was below the pipe and the pipe floated free like an old root. They dug until they saw where the pipe was bent and cracked, where it was rusted red. They picked around the break until they found the thing that had broken it. They stood in their white hats above the hole and looked down into it. Their brown gloves were dirty and they sweated through their shirts. They looked at one another and down into the hole. Afraid and confused, they left. It was 4:45.

After five, the neighbors met around the hole. They peered down and saw a heart. The heart had grown beneath the pipe. The heart slowly beat. Each slow beat pressed against the pipe and moved it.

The elderly woman across the street was disturbed. Word would get out about what had been found underneath the road she had lived on for nearly forty years. Questions would come, questions that she did not know the answer to. How long? What is it? Where does it go? What's it to? How did you not know? What else do you not know? She believed it possible she could still blame the city and the Yazoo clay, but what would happen if she couldn't? What would she do then?

The other next door neighbor, the single woman who spent her nights alone, saw the heart and thought immediately of a wart she once had growing along the edge of her thumb. She was a young girl when the wart grew. It was unsightly—embarrassing if someone ever saw, which they did, Sally Morgan did see it one day at recess. Sally Morgan saw the wart and told and lots of people laughed and asked to see it. The next-door neighbor had been in the bathtub one evening and, the wart softened from the water, she tore into her skin. At the center of the wart was a black seed. In pain, she ripped the seed out, but a few weeks later more warts had grown all around the rim of her thumbnail. She had to go to the doctor to have them burnt off. At school, everyone saw the cartoon-like bandage on her thumb. Look how big it got, they said. To everyone else, it was very funny. To her, it was not. She could still see the scar around her thumb nail. Her ugliness was everywhere.

The young couple felt life emanated from the hole. They set their foldable chairs in front of the hole and watched the heart beating. At night, the street was quiet enough for them to hear it. They took their shoes off and pressed the soles of their feet to the dirt at the lip and felt the heart in their bodies and the heart of the ground beating together. All beat as one, and they held hands and felt each other's heart as if it were the same heart, as if all hearts were the same heart.

The next day came with the trucks again. Men in black suburbans

Schuyler Dickson

stepped out to the hole. The men wore suits and stood around the hole with the white-hatted men. They pointed and talked. They decided to reroute the main line. In the hole with their saws, men sent sparks flying up in the air. The men in suits watched. The heart went on beating. When the piece was finally free, they lifted the heart from the hole. The heart turned gray and its beating slowed. It slowed so much that it finally stopped. "Put it back," one of the men said. But everyone pretended not to hear him.

"We can't put it back," another man said.

Inside their house, the young couple was still barefoot and could feel the heart stop beating in the soles of their feet. They stared out the window and saw the men silently arguing. They watched the men work. More pipe was lowered down. Men wore black masks and welded the metal closed. Before long, a dump truck came and dumped dirt into the hole. They patted the dirt down with the bulldozer blade. The earth shook every time the bulldozer blade slammed against the ground. Once the hole was filled and pressed, the trucks and the bulldozer left.

Things went back to way they had been. Where the hole was was now a long brown mound of dirt that sunk when it rained. When the neighbors saw each other, they nodded and seldom spoke. Sometimes at night, they would dream the same dream. They dreamed that the earth below them opened and called them down into it.

BLOWING THE DAM

We gun it off blacktop onto a small strip of gravel road. Peg-legged truck shaking on the ridge. Early morning moonless-ness. Limbs curve across the windshield, stars behind them gleaming like broken glass. We skid in the truck side-to-side and barrel down the washed out ridge.

In the back of the truck, we've brought what we need. Shot-guns. Tannerite. A trailer loaded with an ATV. The truck feels like a small boat on a storm-ridden sea, and as mountain-sized waves loom and build, all I can do is white-knuckle the sides and hope not to be tossed.

The three of us—Clint, my brother-in-law, Brian, my younger brother, and me, the last three men in our family—are driving on a

Schuyler Dickson

Saturday to our old family land to clear it from beavers. The creek along the edge of the property gets dammed every year or so, and the floodwaters drown the woods and threaten to flood the cabin if the winter rains fall too heavy.

Clearing beavers is a two-step process. In the morning, we blow the dam. In the afternoon, we kill the beavers as they try to rebuild.

Land needs tending. For the ghosts of old to wander, houses need to stand. Killing beavers is a kind of prayer, a lowering of the head to what once was. At least, that's what we tell ourselves.

Clint hops out, unlocks the big metal gate and walks it open as we drive through. The old metal groans as he closes it behind us. It bangs against the post. The sun is coming up, and the warm glow of morning wraps around us.

"God, it's early," Clint says. He unwraps his second bacon, egg, and cheese biscuit from the wrapper. I can hear him chewing it.

"That smells like shit," Brian says.

"It's so damned good. I bet it even smells good to Sammy."

"Not at all," I say.

"Bullshit. You know you would eat it right now if Sarah didn't sniff your breath when you got home. You want a hash-brown?"

"Can vegans eat hash-browns?"

"I'm trying not to die," I say. "Fuck me, right?"

"Everybody dies," Clint says. "Might as well enjoy yourself.

That's what I say."

"That doesn't really smell like enjoyment," I say. "It smells like death."

"Yeah?" Clint says. "Just wait till you smell it later."

The road splits. There's a big lake in the middle of the property, and the road circles on a berm around it. Beer cans sit rusting in the ditch. Shotgun shells are crushed on the road. It's our land, but people poach.

Brian leans forward above the steering wheel to look up at the sky. He's hungover. Bloodshot, swollen eyes. A scar along his chin that he won't talk about. I can smell the night before on him. "Look," he says, pointing.

Above the tree line, two hawks tumble to the earth, embraced and circling, talons latched onto the other. Their bodies plummet. They could hit the ground like that, in embrace. Their deaths wouldn't matter. Nothing would change. We would all forget we even saw them by the afternoon.

My father died last year of a heart attack. He ate steak and drank beer every night of his life. One month after the funeral, I quit eating meat. I quit drinking every night. Brian saw it as a kind of betrayal. "Are we not going to go hunting any more?" he said. "What about fishing? You're not going to eat fish? You can't tell me fish have a soul."

"The mercury," I said. Sarah's mom was having memory problems. The last time I saw her, she didn't know my name.

Schuyler Dickson

"What the fuck are you going to do?" he said.

"I don't know."

Even last week, he tried to rub it in. "I guess it's just me and Clint this year."

"Why's that?"

"That big soft heart of yours."

"It doesn't mean I'm not going to blow up a dam. It doesn't mean I'm out of the family. It doesn't mean I don't have responsibilities."

"Family is a responsibility?"

This is the first beaver clearing without dad, and while his and Mom's house has been cleaned of most of his stuff, the cabin has not. We unload the cooler and the guns from the back of the truck, and it's almost like we're unloading this year on top of last. We forgot to take the trash out last time. In the metal trash barrel are plastic bacon wrappers and Styrofoam trays for meat, beer cans crushed and fading from the sun, Dad's empty can of dip.

We back the ATV off the trailer and stack the canisters of Tannerite, a small explosive, in the back. In the low light it feels like we're moving through water. Clint tips the edge of the hash brown wrapper to his mouth, wads it up, and tosses it into the back of the truck. He opens the cooler and cracks open a beer and guzzles it.

I drive us in the ATV onto the trail near the creek. Water flooded woods. Fallen trees. Huge patches of woods lay bare and open, jagged and splintery like they're piercing the soft belly of sky. Even pines, trees beavers don't usually touch, have thick scrapes of bark gnawed off at the trunks. It's an infestation so bad that I have to remind myself that we came last year, that last year happened at all.

But it did happen. It is happening. I've bailed Brian out of jail twice. The last time, he crashed his truck into an elderly couple's living room and tried to drive off, but the truck got stuck in their flower bed. Each time I bailed him out, on the ride home at six in the morning, him too drunk to talk and his eyes shining dull in the traffic lights, I chewed him out. Think about your wife. Your little girl. It doesn't do any good. Nothing does. I'll get him home and his wife, Ashley, will sit down with me to try to sort him out while Brian goes to sleep in their bed. She bounces their baby girl on her knee and worries.

The three of us really only know each other through our wives. It's like trying to know what's in a windowless building just by looking at the outside: anything could be in there.

Clint cheated on my baby sister, Laurie, three months ago at a work conference in Fairhope, Alabama. I know because Laurie told Sarah. They have a two-year-old named Becky Anne. Laurie's trying to forgive him. They started going to the Presbyterian Church in Brandon that has a Christian-based therapy program. The therapist says they need more Jesus between them, as if that means something. As if that could help. As if anything could be between two people besides space.

Schuyler Dickson

Beavers are tenacious and fruitful. Downstream, beavers make more beavers. Once young beavers come of age, they get kicked out of their home. Resources are too scarce. They go upstream and build their own dams. In that way, they spread themselves against the current. In that way, they're an every-year type of problem.

I'm not immune from problems. I have made a conscious effort to try to be good, thinking that I have spent much of my life not. In short, since dad died, I don't know how to navigate the world of manhood any more. It's an admission that in itself makes me feel queasy. Beforehand, it was easy. Be there for your family, be good at your job. Get drunk, eat steak, have a chew while the game's on. Find your small team and love them.

It hasn't been enough. I have veered toward something else, something bigger, and though I see it as a veering toward, my friends and brothers see me veering away. I am edging close to forty and want do something worthy. It shows itself especially on the tennis court. I don't just want to win. I want my opponent to unravel, to launch balls in frustration over the fence, to feel exposed. I want him to know that the faults in his tennis game are also the faults in his life. Last week, I nearly came to blows with a fifty year old man in knee braces. After he called two of my shots out that were clearly in, I drop-shotted him to the net and sent forehand after screaming forehand directly at his gut. I hit him twice. At set point, I stopped him mid-toss to ask him what the score was. It was a cheap move.

He double faulted and lost the game, refused to shake my hand at the end. Still, in me there is a hope that I showed him what's wrong with himself, that I made the world a little better.

The dam is easy to find. We park along the sour mud of the bank, take the shovels out and begin to dig. With three people instead of four, the work goes slower. It's noticeable and, I'd imagine, on everybody's mind. The dam comes up to about waist high, but it's wide. On the other side, the water builds up and hisses through the sticks.

I try not to think about Brian in his jail cell. Cold metal, blurred vision. The elderly couple sleeping in their beds when his truck barreled through their wall. I try not to think about Clint at his work conference. The drunken sweat. The smell of a stranger's body. His phone accidentally calling my sister in the middle of it. Instead, I try to think of a body suspended in cool water. So deep that it's dark. Soundless.

Twenty pounds of Tannerite go in the holes. We stand far back and Brian shoots.

Sticks and dust explode. Water splatters in droplets across our faces. Rumbling ground beneath our boots. Fire and light. Pluming dust. Small particles that patter in the creek. It's a beautiful feeling: destroying something, taking what is and, through force of will, ending it. Already, water flows through. We smile at each other in the haze. We are brothers again.

Schuyler Dickson

The problem now is that I feel like I live in a zoo. All the old levers of wildness that I used to pull when I was younger turned out to be not levers at all but bars in the cage. Drunken sex, skinny dipping at midnight, all-night binges. The communion they offered was really illusion, isolation.

Brian lights the coals in a chimney and Clint opens up a beer and hands it to me. I drink a sip, wanting to drink back to when drinking made me feel a part of something, not separate. "Cheers," Clint says and raises his beer. We all do. "To James Washington."

"Cheers," we say and we drink. The beer tastes like poison. I can't get around it any more, what it's doing to my insides. I can feel my liver every time I take a sip.

Even achievement has grown tiresome. I coach high school basketball and teach AP Latin at a rich kids' school in Ridgeland. We've won back-to-back state championships even though we're undersized. When my team makes me angry, I blow the whistle and make them run. Their shoes pound the hardwood, their breaths pulse shallow, ragged, and quick. My power doesn't survive seventh period.

In classes, students listen to everything I say, and everything I say comes back to this: power's not good for a person. I talk about Julius Caesar and Marc Antony. I talk about Cato and Brutus. All of their pale, soft faces. Listening, eager to please. Their wide clear eyes. What good is greatness when, like Caesar, a thousand paper cuts can cut a man down on the Senate floor? What good is goodness if an army is outside? What strength is bravery when, like

Cato, all you use it for is to rip out your own intestines? What good is virtue when, like Brutus, all it gives you is a smile as you fall on your sword? And to myself, I ask, what is worthy about life if time doesn't really move until the last second tics by, if all of living is one long march to truly alone?

Brian grills bacon-wrapped dove breasts and jalapenos stuffed with cream cheese. Two Portabello mushrooms for me. Constantly, he opens to lid to look at them, moves the breasts around with his long-handled tongs.

"They're never going to cook if you keep opening it," I say.

"He's cooking them with his eyes," Clint says.

Brian acts like he's handing me the tongs. "You want to cook?"

"You want a crust on it, don't you?"

"If you want to cook, cook. If not, let me do it."

Clint opens another beer and he takes a can of dip out of his front fishing shirt pocket. He takes off the cap and takes a pinch out and puts it in his lip before offering the can to Brian, who takes a small pinch and puts it in his mouth. He jokingly hands it to me.

Brian has a way of drinking a beer like he's biting into it. He's on his fourth of the morning. His mouth opens and the tips of his sharp white canines poke out, and when he drinks his throat opens and he guzzles down a quarter of the can. He tongs the dove breasts and burps quietly. Although it's Fall, the air is warm and sticky, as if

Schuyler Dickson

the blown dam has evaporated and the beaver musk is in our lungs. I'm glad I didn't see any beavers this morning. Beavers are foreign creatures to me, and, to be honest, make me uncomfortable when I see them—their flat tails, their sharp teeth.

"You want another beer?" Clint asks. The one I'm holding is half-full and lukewarm.

"I'm good," I say.

"Here." He stands up off the cooler, opens it, and fishes out another beer. I drain half the lukewarm beer and take the new cold one. I can feel Brian watching me. He wants to say something.

"You got any hot students this year?" Clint asks.

It's a question I get too often from grown men. I used to say, "Jesus, they're children." Now, my canned answer is, "All genius models."

"Haha," he says. "How much do they pay you to say that?"

"Not enough," is my canned answer.

I can feel the beer sloshing around in my belly. It always feels so good at first.

"Brian," I say. I see him looking at me, wanting to say something. "What did you get into last night?" His eyes are red. He didn't sleep.

"Not much," he says. "Stayed home. Watched a movie." Lately, friends will drive by his house on their way to work at five or six in the morning and text me, tell me that they saw him on his front porch, smoking cigarettes and drinking beer. Five in the fucking morning. Used to, I thought he'd be out at the bars. Now, I think he just stays home and drinks while his wife and child sleep.

"One of those all night movies?"

"What's that?"

"Did you watch every Star Wars movie ever made?"

He tongs a few dove over and drops my mushrooms with his fingers onto the grill. He licks his fingers and drinks again. "I watched Braveheart." It was Dad's favorite movie. "I think I watched it twice."

We eat and drink and clean up after ourselves, cramming the beer cans and spit cups and paper plates down the trash barrel. We pile back into the ATV with our shotguns in the back. The leaves are golden and the woods are loud. We park a hundred yards away from the blown dam on the mud of the creek and trek quietly through the bramble.

We split up near the deer stand where Brian killed his first deer, a ten-point buck when he was eight. I remember it only because he still has the picture on the refrigerator, blood smeared on his face. Brian and Clint drift from me in the woods, their gun barrels pointed to the ground.

We set up down the banks of the creek. Though we're all in camo, I can see Brian and Clint's hunter orange glowing behind the trees like two small, foreign suns. Where the dam was, beavers busy themselves with rebuilding. They're everywhere, fifteen to twenty of them. Their brown bodies glisten, and their snouts poke just above the water as they swim their pointed sticks back to their home. They're panicked, traumatized. One stands hunched on the bank near the dam, looking around as if surveying what once was, trying to make its rodent-mind imagine what could have caused this.

A shotgun blasts. Then another. I eye a beaver swimming and fire at it. The shot scatters across the water, and the beaver ducks under. My stomach is electric. My insides are hollow and singing. All around, gunfire explodes.

There on the bank, the same beaver sits, alarmed but still. He hears the gun blasts, tries to picture the old erupted home. He tries to think of how he could have avoided this, what steps he could have taken, what challenges he can lay on his family to keep it from ever happening again.

I fire at him. The beaver tumbles over. The shot tears off a chunk of his wide, flat tail. The animal screams and sits up. It's big. It sniffs its tail and sees me.

Killing never sat well with me. My first deer was a doe. I killed her next to her fawn, who sprinted into the woods when she heard the shot. I didn't cry but I didn't feel joy—not like the joy on Brian's face in the picture—when my father dunked my head in the animal's blood-filled ribcage. I felt cold, absent. I knew nothing of the life I took.

There are other worlds that I can never access. Death is a closed door. To usher it in, to welcome it and run towards it in all its uncertainty—like Dad did, like Brian is doing—is an act of betrayal. A betrayal of the ones they love. A betrayal of life itself.

The beaver's thick, strong neck. Long, yellow teeth. Blood trails after in a dark cloud as it swims across the river. All around, the gunfire booms. Air sulfuric.

My body turns sick with the smell. Downstream, a beaver bursts into a spray of blood and fur. I can see Brian behind a tree, grinning big. It's a vacant, harsh smile, the skin on his face pulled back across his cheeks. Clint cannons dumbly. All is noise. Death is far across the river.

The beaver I shot climbs onto the bank. It charges across the grass. It is fast. I squeeze the trigger and the gun barrel booms. The dirt beside the beaver craters and plumes, splatters into the creek.

"Shit," I hear myself say. The beaver leaps at me. I strafe away, raise the barrel. The beaver's long torso glistens. Its tail is ragged. At once, I feel the weight of its long body career against me, its claws at my calf. It bites into my thigh.

Its eyes are wild and red and depthless. Its head shakes back and forth. Blood seeps out from my skin and torn clothes around its teeth. I grab the beaver behind the neck to try to pull it off. It's in me. All the world is pain and panic. "Help," I say. Beavers lay dying on the creek. The guns blast on.

Its teeth sink further in. I can feel it near the bone. I can't stand. I lay my leg against the ground and beat the barrel of the shot-

Schuyler Dickson

gun against its head. "Help," I'm screaming. "Help me goddamn."

My ears ring. My whole body has gone cold. My shoulder. A piece of it is gone. The shirt is gone. I can smell the gunpowder. The skin is scraped to a smooth crater of blood and muscle. The beaver is gnawing. Blood pools under me. I can smell myself.

Something releases. Brian is there.

His knife is in his hand. His eyes focused and dead. He slashes in one quick movement and stomps the animal against the ground. Over and over, its tiny dying sounds.

I can feel him in the ground. He looks at my shoulder and touches my shirt.

"It's okay," he says, and he looks me in the eye, not side-eyed but whole. When he looks at me, he sees me. When he looks at me, it's as if there is no space between us. "Goddamn. Just hold on. It's okay."

I want to scream. I want time to stop. To end, bleeding on a bank. Clint stands above me. "That's an artery," he says, looking at my leg. The leaves above are washed clean of color. To stay alive precisely here, to never live forward, to never have to remember, to never go away. Their eyes watch. My shoulder, my thigh, bleeding out in the open.

They lay me across the backseat of the ATV. On the bumps, my head bounces on the cushion of the seat, and I can see just outside of the roof to the limbs as they scrape by. It looks as if the limbs are holding on to something. My clothes are heavy, and everything burns. I can hear Brian and Clint talking. "I'm sorry," I try to say. But there's nothing in my throat.

I know what will happen next. The moment is already gone. Today will be another day that we'll never speak of. On crutches, I'll sing in my zoo about the Rubicon. I'll sing of Brutus leaning on his own sword, proud that he could die a good man. I'll sing of Antony leaving his men to be slaughtered so he could go be with the woman he loves. I'll sing it out in the place where nothing changes, wishing I was bleeding on the bank.

Or I will walk through the door, and I'll close it behind me.

Either way, this bank will become another tyrant. I will smell, beneath the drudgery, beneath the stuckness, beneath the grafted skin and blood transfusions, Styrofoam burning in a trash barrel. Where the river runs is the place where nothing is forgotten. All around us the creek is rising. Out in the woods, the water recedes.

Schuyler Dickson

THE SPANGLED

My last true love strapped a homemade bomb to her chest and set herself off this morning, amid the conveyors and catwalks of the ceiling tile factory. She died buried beneath ten feet of pulverized ceiling tile.

Hard as I try, bad as I miss her, all I can remember is her teeth. The news doesn't do anything but show old pictures of her, when her teeth were rotting. Her ex-husband had, in an amphetamine and alcohol rage, cracked the front four out with a crescent wrench. Two months ago, she stole my disability check and went to Dr. Lamkin's to get the gaps filled and the yellow bleached. Beneath the betrayal, I was proud that she went on and did it. It was her last shrugging off of the ugliness of used-to. She was reclaiming her face as hers.

Now I roll around at the roller rink and look in the lights for pieces. Not that they would be there. They would be ghost teeth, but I can't think of anywhere else she would rather have them haunting and sparkling than on the slick floor of the Roll-A-Rena. Even though we couldn't agree on our first date, we could agree on the second. It was at the roller rink, a jokey, low-stakes place where we figured nobody would know us. She wasn't wearing socks so I had to buy her some at the counter. Thick white ones that came up her calf.

"They're warm," she said.

"Those are some good socks. They hug your leg pretty good."

We held hands as the lights lit up the floor and the sound system played. It's the best sound system in town. They played songs we knew and we would skate to the music and even though we were going in a circle it felt like we were going somewhere. Somewhere else, somewhere together.

Now I roll around and moan. My heart's torn out. At the Dairy King in the corner, they have old square televisions mounted near the ceiling. When I whiz by, the screens show old pictures of her yellow teeth. Across the floor, the strobe blinks and the disco ball sparkles like shattered glass. The fog machine kicks on, and for a moment everything is lost in smoke.

I don't know what world I'm living in. I can feel, for a minute, what it would've been like to be her, had she gone on past the blast. The cool smoke rushes under, smelling of vapor and tile. The

Schuyler Dickson

powder's in my skin, she said. She'd itch her calves raw, sometimes on the floor. Neck-tie with his Vaseline on his desk, calling her in, drawing the blinds. "I just want you to know," he said, taking off the Vaseline lid, pointing it at her legs, "there is comfort in this world." He took a big scoop on his curled fingers. "May I demonstrate?"

I don't know what going on looks like if all there is is a circle. Is what she did the Roll-A-Rena's fault? We were heroes as we rolled. We were together and everything was bright. Smoke and booming. Guns unholstered on the video game wall. All of our lives was building up to something. There was in her an itching to do. The movie theatre closed when we were kids. The square's all boarded up. Every building that hasn't closed has a billionaire's name on it. Every one but this one.

"We could always go rolling," I said to her, not knowing who I was talking to any more with her teeth. She got them bleached on the same day she found out the plant was closing. They had been scaling back her hours. Using more contractors. Cut everyone to part-time and canceled their insurance.

"Don't you wonder where all the goodness is at?" she said. She was painting her toenails on the carpet. "With all this nastiness around, don't you want to do something?"

We were watching a cooking show. Giada De Laurentiis with her flat white teeth was making pasta. "You want me to go kick his ass?" I said, meaning her manager. I didn't really want to as I'm opposed to violence and I knew she would say no.

"It's not him." She was talking to me like I had missed an important part of the recipe. "Why's there got to be somebody watching what I'm doing? Why's there got to be a building at all, you know? How come somebody went to designing a building so ugly? How come, it don't matter what I do, it always feels like I'm being looked at but not really being seen?"

I was trying not to look at Giada De Laurentiis. It was hard. She's beautiful and makes beautiful things. Watching her cook made me want to throw on an apron. "A man oughta know not to act that way."

But she was in her toenails. "Who could make a building so ugly? What's going on in their insides?"

There on the screen in the Dairy King is the house where we live together. Yellow tape is wrapped around our tree. A police cruiser has its wheels in my yard. My stupid face comes on the screen. The closed captioning is on, and words scoot across my neck. "Why would somebody do something like this?" the Tupelo reporter asks.

Beneath the TV, the manager of the Dairy King is staring at me, whispering on the phone. I roll around the rink before my limp answer scrolls across. Why does a person do anything, I said. I mean, why buy a Mountain Dew instead of a Gatorade? Why call a friend? Why fall in love? In my experience, a person just does things and then makes up the reasons later.

All of my life, I've felt myself pulled in a single direction, and if I were to look at it from above, I'm sure it'd look like a circle. Like an orbit, maybe, and Sheila was in the middle. Now, there's no center to go around. There's an empty space in the middle of the rink, in the place she used to go and twirl like a figure skater. God, I could watch it all day.

I'd imagine she was a picture of heaven even when she blew herself up.

The strobe light flickers and the green spotlight tracks across the floor. All of the ceiling is washed in sparkle. I'd like to peek into the soul that made the skating rink.

Inspired, I blaze on one wheel through the turn. Behind the ticket counter, the front door opens. The Tupelo reporter and her cameraman step in. They wave at the Dairy King manager in his bolo tie. They set up their camera on the worn carpet near the ski-ball and train the lens on me.

I find it hard to skate while being watched. I consider going to the middle to try to practice the twirl but not if my failure's going to make the ten o'clock news. The tripod follows while I circle. "Excuse me," the reporter says as I cross near her. "Sir? A couple questions?"

Nothing's smooth. The camera makes me feel my limbs. On the TV is a picture of the factory. No one was there when she blew it, not even the manager. A big hole is blown through the side.

I can't stand it. Even the hole is lovely. Everything she touched she left her soul on. I can see clean through the field behind the building. I can see where the sun slants down across the cotton.

"Sir?" the Tupelo reporter says again, but I'm skating away. They pick up their tripod and jog it to the middle of the rink. As I go around, the camera goes around. It can twirl but it's ugly.

"Your insides are rotten," I say. Nothing feels good when I'm getting seen. "Can you even make a marinara?"

All they can do is ask why. Maybe she strapped a bomb to her chest because she wanted to scrape off, like yellow teeth, the ugliness of that factory. Maybe she wanted to spread her beautiful insides out to the world. Maybe she felt that the goodness inside of a person was wasted unless that person did something. Maybe she wanted to show that the factory was just a building. Maybe she just wanted to be seen. I don't know.

All I know is that she was all that ever mattered. Not even the skating rink will do.

"Sir? Please?"

The TV shows her old teeth again.

I skate up to the middle. "That's not the right picture of her," I say, stopping myself with the big rubber knob on the end of my skate. The man hides behind the camera. I can see my mouth upside down in the lens. "It's not right."

"Did she give you any inclination that she could do something like this?" the reporter said. "When did you know your wife was a terrorist?"

I kick the tripod leg.

"Whoa," the reporter says.

Schuyler Dickson

"Show the right picture," I say. I kick the tripod leg again. The leg breaks. The camera tumbles over on its side. The lens shatters and skates across the floor. I grab the cameraman's shirt in both hands and pound my fists against his empty chest. "You've got to show her right. You bastard. You empty-hearted bastard." I shove him, and he falls on his back onto the floor.

Around him, broken glass shines in the strobe like perfect teeth.

OWLS

I heard an owl last night, the old man said.

An owl, his grandson said, feigning interest as he twisted an empty beer can into a thin metal wafer. I'll be damn.

You little shit, the old man said, ringing his cane against the boy's legs. The metal echoed out when the cane struck bone. Watch that little shit-eating mouth. An owl is right.

The boy was seventeen and reached into the cooler next to him on the porch and fished out a cold beer from the ice, side-arming his puck of a can into the front yard, seeing how long it would spin against the concrete.

Some folks scared of an owl, the old man said.

The boy popped the next can open and guzzled. He had had a

Schuyler Dickson

few and they were starting to go down easier. Some, he said.

The old man leaned over his chair, holding his cane by the throat. The brass was notched with an animal's sharp beak. Whooo, the old man said, pointing the beak at the boy's eyes. Whoo whoo.

Knock that shit off.

They're watching, the old man said. Try telling them what you want. Maybe they listen.

You're crazy. He drank the beer until it was half gone. His eyes searched the trees.

Maybe they're listening now. Maybe they hear you. Maybe even if you don't talk, maybe they hear what you think. Maybe they know what you'll do.

Whoo, the boy said, and he laughed a drunken teenage laugh. Whoo whoo.

The owls called back from the branches above them.

See, the old man said.

The boy looked pale.

You know what they want, the old man said but the boy said nothing. That's my seed you got in you. It's the owl seed. The owls want to spread themselves.

I told you, the boy slurred. Becky Cochran don't want nothing to do with me.

We'll see, the old man said. Whether you're a man. Or a coward. What do you say?

Don't call me a coward.

That's what your momma said, too.

There was a party that night at someone at school's deer camp. Behind a small building was a clearing with a bonfire. Kids stood around the fire drinking and smoking and talking in groups. One drunk boy was walking on top of the burning pallets while everyone else watched and cheered. Sparks flew up around his legs like crackling stars.

The boy, Sean, sat on a cooler and looked at everyone. Near the building, sitting on the steps, was Becky Cochran. She had clean dark hair and was holding a can of beer with two hands as if she were warming it, talking intently about some personal injustice or other. Everything that happened with pretty people seemed to Sean to happen at high volume. He envied it.

Scooch, someone said and hit his knee. It was Claire. He scooted over and she sat on the cooler with him so their sides touched.

When did you get here, she asked.

Just now. What about you.

Like an hour ago. It sucks. I wish there was somewhere else to go.

You want a beer?

Yeah but I don't want to get up. Give me a sip of yours.

He handed her his beer and she drank from it and he watched the can touch her lips.

Hey don't drink it all, he said and reached to take it away from her.

Stingy, she said, and she popped him on the shoulder. Did you drive here?

No. You?

I rode with Leslie. God, I'm so bored.

He drained the rest of the beer and looked at Becky, how she nodded gravely while the girl she was talking to validated her. Exactly, he watched Becky mouth.

Beautiful people like Becky seemed to live on a different planet. They had been given maps to life, and when they looked at the maps everything made sense. Teachers were kinder. Tests were easier.

Claire put her head on his shoulder. I bet Leslie could catch a ride with Pete. I know she likes him.

Yeah?

I could drive us. I've just had a couple.

He could feel her hair on his neck. Where we gonna go, he said.

I don't know, she said. I don't care. Anywhere.

They drove around for hours, talking about the party and the people they knew. He liked her. And she liked him. She told him so as they lay on the hood of the car on a curve in the road that looked out over a cornfield.

I'm so glad you moved here, she said.

Yeah, he said. Their shoulders touched, their hips. Above they watched a satellite track by. She propped herself up on her elbow.

I felt like nobody really understood me until you moved here.

Yeah.

Seventeen years of having nobody understand you. That's crazy, isn't it.

I don't know if it's so crazy.

How come you never talk about your parents? How come you never talk about Meridian?

I don't know. I guess I don't know what to say.

You can talk to me if you want.

I know. I like talking to you.

She smiled. Good.

Why don't you come home with me. Spend the night.

Your grandpa won't care?

He only cares about what he wants to care about. He won't say anything.

I don't know.

Your parents expect you home?

It's not that. They think I'm out with Leslie.

You don't have to. We don't even have to do nothing. I just thought it'd be nice to spend the night together. But it's okay. We can just sleep on the car hood if you want. I don't know, maybe that's what you're into. You into sleeping on car hoods?

She smacked him on the arm. It's not so bad on a car hood, she said. I bet we're leaving two big butt prints on it.

Schuyler Dickson

Leslie's gonna be mad.

Stop.

She'll probably kill you.

Oh my god. She will not.

She'll probably kick your ass at least. I've seen her, she's got that look.

She's like the sweetest person in the world. Like really.

Nobody's gonna kill you if you leave butt dents in my bed.

She laughed. Okay.

Nobody.

All right.

Not a soul.

The old man's name was Clyde but he didn't go by that. He tried for a long time not to go by anything, reasoning that there were two options in this world that might benefit a person—to develop a name that got a person entry into places that were otherwise closed or to not have a name at all and to slink like a vapor where one willed himself to slink. But he had found some years ago that even vapor couldn't get through ceilings.

And though he was old, the new name he chose would go on forever. Seed needed to be planted in fertile ground, and for far too long his seed had been cast into clay. Meredith, his daughter, the boy's mother, hadn't wanted to cooperate. He had picked her out a preacher in Meridian, a young man the church was grooming for bigger things. But she went off and married that peckerhead who had his head so stuffed with action movies that he went and joined the army and died in the desert halfway around the world for a reason he didn't care enough to know about.

Meredith, after the peckerhead died, was caught in a state of inertia that, hard as Clyde tried, she wouldn't shake herself free of. He devised plans, steps to pull them all out of the lean gray suffering of poverty and into a new day where their name when spoken would wallop.

But when a person close to another person is caught in inertia, everything around them begins to die. Like a diseased tree, if the disease isn't treated the whole orchard will droop and decay. And so thankfully, late one night in their yard, the owls came and popped their beaks into her skull, and now he and the boy were living again.

The boy was dumb but different than his mother. He wouldn't be so caught up in the name of his country, in the tingle of a uniform and purpose. The old man had ruminated and the fruits of his rumination claimed that salvation wasn't won in the pulpits of grace but in the patrol car of power. The ultimate rule is that kin protected kin, but, beyond that, kin created community and community created power and instilled that power in symbols and bestowed those symbols to those that it felt were worthy.

Give the boy a sheriff in his line, and what stepping stone might lie just beyond?

So it was with these thoughts that the old man went to wake

Schuyler Dickson

the boy up Sunday morning. He had found where the Sheriff prayed, where he dragged his family to sing and be seen singing, and it was his intent to like a wolf enter into the pasture.

He pushed open the boy's door without knocking. And although it was dark behind the pulled curtains, he could see in the bed a young woman. Bile rose in the old man's throat. He caned to the side of the bed and watched them sleep. The girl's tits were out of the covers, and the old man watched them knowing that there was only one direction that tits went.

He struck them both with the ball of his cane. Whore, he said. Harlot. He hit them across the chest and against their hips. Get up, he said. They jumped up and covered their heads with their arms. The girl screamed. The boy tried to cover her body with his. You poor no named piece of shit, the old man said, hearing the thud and smack of the round ball against bone and skin. You fucking emptiness. You fucking void. You're planting your seed to rot in sand. Get out. Go.

Hellfire, the boy said, until he managed to grab the cane.

The old man leaned into the boy's face. Get up. Put your church clothes on. Brush that whore out your mouth.

For two months, the old man dragged the boy to every event that the Second Baptist Church had, every potluck luncheon and prayer breakfast, every Sunday school and both morning church services where the old man would half sing and half growl through the hymns in his suspenders and his slicked back hair, his cane hanging on the pew in front of him by the cane's pointed hook.

Instead of singing, the boy would stare at the dull shine on his grandfather's cane. That cane was his god, he believed, and he was subject to its rule. He hated the cane: for how his grandfather had hit him with it since he was a boy, yes, but also how it begged him to fashion something similar one day—something edged with a blade maybe—and inflict its control on his grandfather and finally free himself. How the cane called for either his complete subjugation or the will to escalate to violence. He asked himself as the preacher droned on whether he was a coward or not. Wondered how a person could even know.

The old man had forbidden him from seeing Claire, but at school he devised ways to see her as often as possible. She dual-enrolled at the community college for some of her classes, so he went to the counselor to see if he could join her but the counselor said it was too late to sign up. He could, though, sign up for advanced math, and that would mean they could share not just one class but also a study hall.

For two periods every school day, he was happy. He would watch her from across the room in math class when the teacher was at the board, and Claire would glance back and smile at him, waving her fingers on her desk in a small wave that was meant only for him. In study hall they would share a table, and when their hands touched, their fingers would hook together underneath the table and rest on her lap. She'd share her math homework with him and he would stare

Schuyler Dickson

sometimes at the way her numbers looped so cleanly on the page.

It was the same loopy handwriting he saw when she slipped him a note one study hall.

We need to talk, the note said.

About what, he scribbled back.

In person, she wrote.

The intercom popped on. Teachers, please excuse this announcement.

We can't, he wrote, I told you.

We're pleased to announce this year's Who's Who Beauty and Beau Court.

Just write it, he wrote.

She looked around and mouthed something to him, but he couldn't hear what it was. His name was read from the loudspeaker. People in study hall were looking at him.

What's that, he said.

Claire smiled at him. Congratulations, she said.

Becky Cochran's name was read out loud. The name alone made him queasy.

Quiet, the study hall coach said.

What is it, he whispered.

Like a beauty pageant, Claire wrote.

Claire's name was read out from the speaker.

Her face turned white.

Hey, congratulations, he said. He squeezed her knee but she

wasn't smiling.

Quiet, the coach said.

What's the matter, he whispered. He wrote on the slip, tell me.

She took the slip of paper, tore off a small corner, and jotted something down. She slid the piece of paper in front of him underneath her thumb. She lifted up her thumb enough for him to see one word: pregnant.

You are, he mouthed.

She slid the piece of paper back and wadded into a ball and put the ball in her mouth under her tongue. She raised her hand.

Coach Lewis, she said. Can I go to the bathroom?

Is it an emergency, he said.

Yes sir.

She got up and left. He didn't see her for the rest of the day.

The old man drove them to Bible study that afternoon. They sat in metal foldout chairs in the parish hall while Sheriff Cochran read from Genesis, the story about Jacob wrestling with God in the dark of Jacob's tent. The old man imagined himself worthy, in full-throated conflict with the divine, struggling in a dense dark fog of sweating and panting before he pinned his God's arms back and mounted Him and cackled in His face.

When the talk was over the old man jerked the boy by the arm and caned over to the Sheriff as he was talking with his wife

Schuyler Dickson

near the refreshment table. The old man took a powdered donut and set it on a small napkin and touched the tip of his tongue to the powder before eating the small donut whole and he took a cup of unsweet tea from the lines of cups already filled, the ice melting and floating at the top in slivers. The boy could hear him take every bite and gulp.

Say, Sheriff, the old man said, so loud that some nearby turned and looked. Quite the homily, he said, sticking his hand out and grabbing the sheriff's arm as if to hold him there. Mighty fine. I love a man that talks about stories. Them's too many that talks about verses. One line here and one line there. No sir. Give me a story, that's how you get to the truth.

Thank you, the sheriff said. I appreciate that.

And your fine daughter, the old man said. Where is she this afternoon.

The sheriff's wife said, there was a basketball game she had to cheer at.

Oh cheering at basketball games, the old man said. Who would of thought that cheering at a basketball game might wreck a young man's heart. She's about all my grandson can talk about. She's the whole reason he's been coming to church to tell you the truth. At first I thought I made a Christian out of him, but now I know it wasn't me. Your daughter's saving souls, Sheriff. So what's a matter, boy. Ask what you come up here to ask.

He felt the boy stiffen next to him.

He's shy, the old man said. He'd like to take your daughter on a date one time. To the movies, up in Tupelo maybe. Some ice cream if there's a decent ice cream place there. What do you say? Your daughter's been making a good Christian out of him.

Oh, the sheriff's said, I don't know. She has a boyfriend that might not be too happy. A college boy. Sigma Chi.

Boyfriend, the old man said. Pah. She's a teenage girl. I've seen it happen, all my life almost. Heck it happened with my daughter to tell the truth, God rest her soul, the boy's momma, and it's something I regret every day. A girl'll latch on to a boy so quick that she don't see that there's a whole world out there. I've seen it with my own eyes. She's too pretty for that. She's too kind. And it's just a movie, nothing else. Maybe they don't get along but then everybody knows. That's what I like, just knowing the truth. You seem like a man that likes to know the truth.

Then he looked at the boy. Friday, he said, that's what you had in mind right?

The boy could feel the old man's fingers digging into the bone of his arm. The boy nodded.

What's that, the old man said.

Yessir, the boy said.

He's a good boy, the old man said to them. He just got picked to be on the beauty court. Not even here a whole semester yet and they voted him up on the beauty court. Now how bout that. Him not knowing a soul, not a momma around, his daddy dead in the Gulf War and all of that and still. I'll be the first to say I'm proud.

Schuyler Dickson

That's something, the sheriff's wife said.

Yes it is. So what do you say.

I'll talk to her about it, the sheriff's wife said. Certainly.

Oh of course. I'm sure she'll love to. He'll pick her up after school on Friday.

Well let me make sure she doesn't have plans first, the sheriff's wife said.

She has lots of plans, the Sheriff said.

No plan but God's plan, the old man said. If there's one thing I learned it's that. God laughs at man's plans.

Isn't that the truth, the sheriff's wife said and they all laughed.

Claire wasn't at school the next day or the day after that. Sean floated through the classes like an empty can. He'd stare at her vacant desk and try to imagine her there but imagining didn't do much but make the empty desk somehow emptier.

That afternoon, he drove to Tupelo to the mall to get fitted for the tuxedo he'd have to wear for Who's Who. The seamstress was a rough, careless woman who pinched him and touched his hip and shoulder and in-seam with measuring ribbon. He didn't want to go but for the image of standing on the stage with her, winners, just the two of them smiling out at the applause. She would hold flowers and have her hand looped into the crook of his arm. That and only that, he felt, would make his grandfather see her worth, make him believe that the

OWLS

OWLS   147 two of them could be together.

That night he ate a bologna sandwich and drank beer in front of the TV. The old man was in his easy chair, his cane between his legs and both hands perched on the ball and beak at the top of the cane, using the cane to rock himself back and forth and stare out the windows to the overgrown back yard. When it got dark, an owl came and perched on the limb of the big oak tree. It peered into the house, and the old man peered right back, rocking, his mouth moving.

The boy dragged his cooler out to the front yard and lined his empty cans up in the driveway. He sat on a camping chair on the porch and shot his pellet gun at the cans, tearing the aluminum and imagining it was the skin of something ancient and horrible. The more he drank the more cans he could kill. By midnight the driveway was littered with shredded metal.

When he went back inside, the old man was waiting for him.

Sit down, the old man said. The den was dark.

I can't see, the boy said.

You don't need to see. You need to listen.

The boy stumbled. He was drunk but trying to hide it.

The old man said, the only gift God ever gave me was meanness. Our station in life is sorry. Power doesn't get shared, boy. It gets taken. And to take another person's power, you have to use your gifts and you have to be protected. By money or by kin. Do you understand?

Yessir.

Schuyler Dickson

The only gift God gave you is prettiness. Do you know what God does to those who squander their gifts?

Yessir.

What?

I don't know.

They burn. They burn for all eternity. Now burning I don't mind. I've resigned myself to it. But eternity either way seems its own damnation if the seed that fell from my loins withers in the same rot that raised me. Now listen. You're slow and you're drunk so listen to me and remember. I want you to fuck that girl. I want you to give her a child, I want you to give the Sheriff a grandchild, something he'll have to use his power to protect. I want you to join our family and theirs. And I want to use my gift for the good of us all. But it won't work, none of it will work, if you don't fuck that girl. Do you hear me?

Yessir.

Do you understand?

I do.

Good. Now go to bed.

But I don't have to.

The old man sat there and seethed.

What did you say, the old man said.

Claire. The girl you saw me with. The girl you hit. She's pregnant.

What did you say?

We have a line now. It's the same plan. It's just with Claire and not Becky Cochran. I don't even know Becky Cochran.

The same plan, the old man spat. He jumped up from his chair and he struck the staff of the cane across the boy's shoulder. The boy had never been hit so hard. It knocked the breath out of him.

The old man leaned into the boy's face. The boy could smell his acrid breath. You listen to me, you little shit, the old man said. You'll do exactly what I say. And if you don't, the owls will come. And the owls will kill you. Like they killed your momma. Do you understand?

Yessir.

After class one day, he asked his advanced math teacher, Mrs. Sherman, if she knew where Claire was.

Oh, honey, Mrs. Sherman said. She didn't tell you? I think she has the flu.

He called her house when he got home but no one answered.

What are you doing, the old man said.

Nothing. Just making a phone call.

Come here.

What is it?

I want to show you something.

He followed the old man down the barren hall. Pictures lay in shallow boxes on the floor. They still hadn't finished unpacking.

Outside, in the driveway, was a black Ford Mustang. It was

Schuyler Dickson

clean and shiny with a yellow racing stripe down the hood, after-market rims and a spoiler.

You bought this for me? the boy said.

I bought it but there's a fourteen day return policy. It's yours for the night, though. You can do whatever you want in it. Here.

The old man handed the boy the keys. Start her up, he said.

The boy climbed in the front seat and started the engine. It was a clean and easy start. He mashed the accelerator down and listened to it hum.

My life's in your hands, the old man said. All of our lives. Mine. Your mother's. Your sand-choked daddy. They're suffering now, wanting a reason to endure. There, he said, pointing his cane to the backseat, dwell all the eyes and hopes of your burning kin.

After school, the boy drove around in the car. He wanted to drive it around the country roads nearby but didn't want to get it dirty, so he drove to town and revved it at stop lights and circled Becky Cochran's neighborhood near the golf course, drinking one beer to try to make his head stop beating.

He parked on the street because a black SUV took up the driveway. The windows were tinted black. It was, he thought, her father's work vehicle. He had seen it at school.

He didn't have flowers and felt dumb. He had the car, though, which somehow made him feel more foolish than he already was, like he was wearing clothes two sizes too big. He stood at the door and breathed and mashed the doorbell and when no one came he beat his fist against the door.

A small-sounding dog barked inside. He heard heavy footsteps and the door opened. Sheriff Cochran was there.

Is Becky home, the boy said.

The Sheriff looked at him. She is, he said.

I'm here to pick her up.

Is that your car?

Yessir.

The Sheriff opened the door and walked out, closing it behind him. Is it a V6, he asked.

I don't know.

Look, the Sheriff said. I'm going to be honest with you.

He walked down the sidewalk toward the car. The boy followed him, unsure of whether to follow behind him or walk in the grass.

I like you, the Sheriff said. I like seeing you and your old man at church. But I just don't know you. And Becky, she just doesn't know you. And I'm not trying to hurt your feelings or insult you or your old man or anything, but I just don't feel comfortable having my daughter get in a car with someone she doesn't know. Someone I don't know. Does that make sense?

Yessir. I understand.

Good. But that don't mean you can't get to know somebody. It just takes a little while is all.

That's why I was thinking we would go to the movies. To get to know each other.

The Sheriff walked around to the back of the car like he was inspecting it. Is this a rental, he asked.

No sir.

It's got rental plates on it.

We bought it from a rental place I guess.

Hmm.

You can get a good deal that way.

Oh I understand. Pop the hood for me. I want to see.

The boy climbed in the driver's side and looked around for the latch. He couldn't find it.

Check the floorboard, the sheriff said. Or right under the dash.

The boy found it and pulled the lever and the hood popped up. He watched the Sheriff through the front windshield, thinking how easy it would be to throw the car in drive and run him over. To run go get Claire and get the hell away from the old man, from everything.

Start it up for me, the Sheriff said. Stay in there. I want you to gun it.

The boy started the engine and pressed the accelerator down. He thought about Claire. He thought of the child inside her and how he was going to love it. The hood slammed shut and the driver's side door closed and the Sheriff was leaning there in the open window.

No sir, I don't think she's going to be coming out today. She just doesn't want to, and you're going to have to be okay with that. You and your old man. Do you understand?

Yessir.

Good. You're a good young man. Now go on. We'll see you at church this week.

The boy drove off, humiliated and relieved. He drove to the only gas station outside of town that sold him beer and bought a twelve pack. He rode around and drank three and started feeling both worse and better. He was trapped and had always been trapped and he could not imagine any way out until, finally, the image became clear in his head. He would pick up Claire in the Mustang and together they would ride far away.

No, there was nowhere to go. Wherever he went, owls watched and hunted and called while the rest of the world slept.

For the first time in his life, the boy felt the ceiling and walls around him, and for the first time, he blamed the Sheriff. Maybe the old man was right. His station in life was set, and the only way to alter it was by the use of force.

But speed was its own kind of force. Maybe he could run away. If he left now, right now, picked up Claire and drove in one direction, the old man wouldn't even start looking for a day or two. If he were gone all night, the old man would think the boy and Becky were together somewhere. He wouldn't even begin to look until morning.

Schuyler Dickson

It was dark when he pulled up to Claire's house, a gray, ranch-style building in the neighborhood near the school. He saw her car parked in the driveway, SENIORS scrawled in bright pink on the back windshield. He drove by and then circled the neighborhood and drove by again, hoping to see her outside or in a window. But the house was dark, all but for the blue flickering light of a TV against a wall.

Instead of stopping, he drove to the field where they had gone together, the same field he thought he would take Becky Cochran. There, he drank and listened to music and watched the corn until the corn was ugly to him. He stayed until morning, and then he went home, where the old man was waiting.

Well, the old man said.

I did it, the boy said.

What do you mean you did it.

I fucked her.

The old man looked at him. Are you drunk.

Yeah, she likes to drink.

Sometimes it doesn't take the first time.

We did it a few times.

Youth can, the old man said. Still, sometimes the first few times it won't take. You'll have to do it again.

Okay.

One night's not enough. And you need to quit jacking off.

I said okay.

Don't you walk away from me. Listen. A boy becomes a man when he finds that he can act on the world and that the world bends to his will.

Okay. Good.

The old man grabbed the boy by the shoulders and looked into his red eyes.

Inside is the owl's will, he said. If the owl wants a mouse, a mouse appears. He is always looking. And he is always finding what he's looking for. The owl creates lack so he can feel gratification. A life without hunger is a life not worth living. A life of only hunger is an owl choosing to nest in hell.

At school the next Monday, he saw Becky Cochran talking with a small group of girls. He heard her say, "He drove to my house. My dad had to go outside and run him off." They laughed uncontrollably, and throughout the rest of the day, everyone that looked at him had a small pitiful smile on their face.

At break, outside the baseball field at a small concrete picnic table, he saw Claire. He took his Gatorade and went and sat by her. She was pale. She had dark circles around her eyes.

You been sick, he said.

She nodded. She had been crying.

Mrs. Sherman said you had the flu.

Well Mrs. Sherman was right, she said.

You okay?

She nodded her head.

Hey, he said. You all right?

Did you try to take Becky Cochran out on a date?

What?

That's what she's telling everybody. That her dad had to run you off.

No. I mean, my grandfather made me. I didn't want to do it.

Asshole, she said.

She stood up, wadding the lunch bag that held her sandwich into a ball.

Everyone's laughing at you, she said. You know that, right?

I don't care. I didn't want to.

You are such a fucking idiot.

She threw the plastic ball at him. It hit him in the chest and fell to the concrete.

I've been trying to talk to you for like a week.

Why.

I wanted to ask you to go to the Who's Who dance with me.

Go ask Becky Cochran. Go right now and do it. I want to watch her laugh in your face. I want to watch everyone laugh at you, you fucking asshole.

The old man drove alone to Who's Who. He had pressed his shirt and put pleats in his pants and slicked his hair back like he had for church. He sat in the bleachers of the hot, dark gym. On the floor of the basketball court, a stage had been constructed. A black backdrop with glittery stars and a cardboard moon.

The old man's attendance there was humiliating. Watching the parade of sequin-skinned girls and boys with ties and backwards baseball caps march by and pose, each selected for things like "Wittiest" and "Most Likely to Succeed."

Across the gym, the old man saw the Sheriff sitting with his wife. Next to them both, a young man. The boy didn't look like the Sheriff's son. The boyfriend, the old man thought.

At the end of the program, his grandson appeared on the stage. The old man didn't realize it, but the boy was in a beauty contest. There were judges. The boys presented themselves and turned and the girls presented themselves and turned. He watched with interest as the boy, now a piece of the old man, was judged and made the top five. So too did Becky Cochran. So too did the little trollop whom he beat in the bed, the one who was pregnant with the old man's great grandchild. The girl, he saw, was glowing.

The boy, he saw, was drunk. The old man could tell not because they boy was stumbling but because the boy was upright, tall and confident, smiling.

Five boys and five girls stood across the stage. They were beautiful now, but time worked on beauty harder than it worked on anything else, harder than titles and mind and soul and will. All that we worship never lasts. Nothing but power.

Ladies and gentleman, the emcee said.

Schuyler Dickson

The old man despised the emcee.

Our most handsome and most beautiful. Sean Lacy. Becky Cochran.

The old man knew. He had willed it. The two walked forward on the stage. The boy was given a crown. The girl was given flowers.

But something was wrong. Something was happening that the old man hadn't willed. Becky Cochran was blushing. The other contestants were smirking. The boy pushed his hands together as if he were crushing an imaginary can. He slouched now, shoved his hands into his pockets and hung his neck, as if the crown was too heavy.

The old man looked across the gym. The Sheriff was angry. The boy next to him was pale. Upset.

Becky Cochran smiled at the camera. She shook her head and turned around and looked at her friends and mouthed, oh my god.

This is not what young lovers did. The boy had told him a lie. The boy was being laughed at. The old man was being laughed at. He felt the owl in his chest begin to flutter.

His breath would be owl breath. His eyes would be owl eyes. The old man sat in his seat and watched the crowd file out of the gym, watched the Sheriff and the Sheriff's family sitting together, smiling, accepting hugs from the people around them. So beautiful, he would see them mouth. He would never catch the Sheriff alone. Men like that were never alone. They couldn't stand solitude, silence, what voice might appear in the quiet of their minds.

When the boy came out on the floor holding his tuxedo on the hanger draped across his shoulder, he walked slumped and alone behind the stage. The crown dangled from the hanger hook, cheap plastic and sequins that didn't sparkle anywhere but under big lights. The old man caned down to the floor, the metal ball sweating in his hands, the point protruding between his index and middle fingers.

Come on, the old man said. The boy followed behind him.

Did you see I won? the boy said.

I saw it, the old man said. I saw it all. Give me the keys.

They climbed in the car together and the old man started the engine. He felt his belly rumble. The boy held the plastic crown in his lap.

The thing about a crown, the old man said. It don't mean anything if you don't use it.

It's not even real, the boy said.

Everything's made of something.

He reversed out of the parking space and almost hit someone. He put the car in drive and heard someone tap against the back of the car. The old man stopped.

The Sheriff stood at the window.

The old man rolled the window down, smiling the biggest smile the boy had ever seen from the old man.

You must be one happy daddy, the old man said. She looked beautiful. Like a princess.

Schuyler Dickson

You should be too, the Sheriff said.

He pointed across the seat. The boy sat there pale, petrified.

I just wanted to make sure, the Sheriff said, that there weren't no hard feelings. A man's only daughter, he's got to look out for her. You understand.

The old man took the Sheriff's hand and squeezed. I understand, he said. Believe me, I understand everything.

When they got home, the boy threw his tuxedo and the crown on the back of the couch and went to the refrigerator and took out a six pack of beer and sat on the back patio and looked out at the trees where the moon shone down. The old man watched him from inside, saw the light catch a speck of glitter on the top of his head where the plastic crown had set.

After a while, the old man went outside. The boy sat in his chair and the old man stood over him. The girl, he said, the one you got pregnant. You love her.

The boy laughed a small, dry laugh.

She lives by the school, the old man said but the boy didn't say anything. He was frozen, as if the weight of the plastic crown had broken his neck.

Answer me.

That's right.

The old man was holding his cane tightly.

You lied to me, he said.

Shit, the boy said.

You lied to me, he said again, and he shook the armrests of the boy's chair. He bent down into the boy's face. Terror was in his eyes, in his weak, childish, drunken eyes.

Your mother lied to me. And you know what happened?

I'm so sick of hearing about that damned owl.

Don't you talk that way.

It's how I talk.

The boy smiled a drunken, wide smile.

I'm the king now, the boy said.

The king, huh, the old man said.

I got me one, the boy said. A real crown.

Here's your crown, the old man said. The old man swung the cane down onto the boy's head. The ball and point landed with a thud that the old man could feel inside his shoulder socket. The boy was still smiling that childish smile as he lay on the concrete, as blood pooled out from the hole in his head. The old man watched the boy's red face turn pale. He watched him as he died, seeing the same quivering mouth that he saw on the boy's mother when he had killed her too.

The old man looked the girl's name up in the phone book and drove to the neighborhood near the Country Club. He found a house with a car in the driveway that had SENIORS on the back windshield. He pulled into the driveway and caned up to the front door, and he knocked. Lights were on in the den where a TV flickered.

The door opened. Claire answered.

Hello? she said.

My grandson, the old man said. He needs you.

Tell him I don't want to see him.

He's been hurt, the old man said.

What? the girl said. Is it bad?

Come with me, the old man said. He needs you.

The girl stepped out into the night and closed the door behind her. She crossed her arms in front of her chest.

Is he okay? Is he in the hospital?

She followed him down the steps, down the driveway. The old man's cane was warm in his hand, as if it were living, breathing, guiding.

I know what's inside you, the old man said.

What, she said.

The old man opened the door.

He told me, the old man said. And I'm going to protect you. That's me inside you.

It was an accident, she said.

It's okay. It'll be fine. Just get in.

The girl climbed in. The old man saw her, glowing in the light, as he slammed the door, and she was beautiful.

ASSES

1.

Now is a small concrete room. Then is a dull gray fog of misremem-
brance and tastes long-turned sour, cotton-mouth and eyes so used to
sleep they can't quite open.

Now, narrow, enclosed bunks are mounted on the walls.
Small lights blink on control panels. The glass lids of two bunks are
open.

"How well did you know your mother?" Lefty asks.

"How well did I ever know anybody?" Pancho says. "I don't
even know myself."

They told me their real names once, but I can't remember.

"If a man comes to know himself, he's come to see himself

Schuyler Dickson

both outside and inside, comes to know himself like his mother knows him, and now by knowing himself he knows his mother."

They sit on stools in the middle of the room. The lights blink and a machine whirs.

Lefty remembers something but considers it like he's chewing a bite too big. "I'm remembering something. Yes, I can see it now, my only memory. Seventh grade civics class. Coach Godwin writes the word 'assume' up on the board. Draws a line between the 's' and the 'u' and then another between the 'u' and the 'm.' You see where this is going. I don't even have to finish."

"I don't follow."

"He says, 'when you assume, you make an ass out of u and me.'"

"Still not there."

Lefty draws it with his finger in the air. Ass|u|me.

"I see. His mother's pride. In both coital bliss and guttural grunts where she pushed him from one world to another—"

"As if that was some kind of goal."

"I constantly go between worlds. I mean like always."

"I am in the in-between."

"One world mothers another."

"I can't talk about this anymore."

"There, the sweat on her brow, both times strangely something lodged in her canal."

"What goes in must come out."

"There, like in the movies, she gets a glimpse of truth and the future."

"The what?"

"The future. And it is there. Her son. Grown. Standing at a chalk board in front of eighth grade(?), seventh grade(?) minds. Yes, she thinks. My labor will add up to something. And she hears him explain it. What? What's the matter?"

"Some of the words you use."

"She sees her son there. And what does she think? That it's all worth it?"

"It's not worth it?"

"What is 'it?'"

"You haven't learned your lesson. Who is the ass now?"

"Who is the ass still?"

"But wait. Maybe one child in the room nodded gravely and understood. And from then on, assumed nothing. Where would that person be today?"

"All along? I was the ass?"

"You and me."

"Look."

"What?"

Lefty stares at a bunk. He tilts his head like he's listening. "I thought I saw one move."

They both look.

"Which one?"

Schuyler Dickson

"Shh."

"Nothing's moving."

"We were once like that."

"Not moving?"

"I assume."

"There we go."

"Oh wow. Again. All this time."

"Go over it again."

"What?"

"What you remember."

"I only have the one memory."

"No. Just a little while ago. When you woke up."

"I told you like five minutes ago."

"I've forgotten pieces."

"So I tell you again and you forget again."

"I won't forget this time."

"Why tell it again?"

"The facts. If here we are not making assumptions in an attempt to save ourselves from assery, then we need to discuss facts and facts only."

"Just the facts, ma'am."

"What?"

"I was pretending to be a detective."

"Are you a detective?"

"I don't know."

"But some kind of military."

"It's really anyone's guess at this point. Maybe I changed careers while we were sleeping."

"A person can do that?"

"I make no assumptions of a person's limitations."

"You've seen a person do that?"

"I perhaps saw myself do it. I was once a detective. I woke up. Now I am—"

"Are we not still detectives?"

"I guess I'll always be one."

"So you haven't changed at all."

"I don't know."

"A person gets killed either way."

"For what?"

"For changing, for not changing. 'You're not the man I married.'"

"Who said that?"

"An imaginary conversation I'm having. 'You've changed.'"

"We are having a real conversation, and you've aborted our real conversation for an imaginary one?"

"Or you can hear this one: 'We've all grown up but so-and-so's stayed the same.'"

"How exactly should a person be for these imaginary friends?"

"They don't seem like friends, do they?"

Schuyler Dickson

"But they're you."

"Let's not talk about them. Where were we?"

"I don't know, detective."

"You were filling me in."

"I was not."

"I was telling you I won't forget this time."

"So you said."

"Please."

"I could be lying."

"But you wouldn't, would you?"

"I don't know. It could be a lie implanted in my head by the voices that tell us we have both changed too much and not changed enough."

"Abandoned our good qualities. Embraced the badness."

"Embraced our asses."

"The ass is a curious instrument."

The lights flicker and another memory strikes. Lefty leaps up. "Another memory. Same time period. A boy sat on stage at the Family Life Center at the First Baptist Church, lay on his back, grabbed his knees to his chest, and farted on command. Over and over. 'How do you do that?' someone asked. 'I suck air in through my butthole,' he says."

"More like that and we'll finally know who we are, finally know if we've changed for the better or worse or not at all."

"It must be one of those three."

"But back to the ass. Is it enough to know what we consist of? What does an ass consist of?"

"This one I know. The skin, the muscle, the crack."

"We're missing something."

"Those are all the parts."

"The hole?"

"How can a hole be a part of something?"

"True. The ass is divided into two parts. But the ass is still singular. Even though we have two?"

"It's still just the one. The crack is a part of the singular ass."

"How can an absence be a part of something?"

"It is the crack that defines an ass."

"When we talk about ass, are we not talking about empty space?"

"If an ass comes to know its crack, it has come to know itself."

"Is that what was on the robot that came in here?"

"What?"

"Did it measure our ass cracks? Then show on the screen the length and width in millimeters?"

"What screen? I thought you said you didn't remember."

"I don't remember. That's why I am asking."

"No. It wasn't an ass crack measurement."

"But he did take a measurement."

"He?"

"The robot."

"You didn't tell me there was a robot last time."

"I guess I forgot."

"What did it say?"

"It didn't say anything."

"What did it do?"

"It, like, scanned us. Its eyes lit up. It was blinding."

"It scanned us. Yes. Of course. We were sleeping together?"

"No. I was in that bunk and you were in that one. I woke up and it was scanning me. I saw on a screen or something. 'Item Found: 100 lb Potatoes.'"

"It thinks you're potatoes? Did it scan me? What did it think I was?"

"It said, 'Object Not Detected.'"

"I'm a stowaway?"

"It's clearly faulty."

"That's an assumption."

"I am obviously not potatoes. You are obviously very much detected. I am detecting you as I speak."

"You could be faulty. You could be a faulty potato sack."

"True."

"I could be the imagination of a faulty potato sack. How would one know?"

"One wouldn't."

Silence.

"I have a vague vision of potatoes coming not in sacks but boxes."

Silence.

"Did you know your mother?"

Silence.

Lefty stands and stretches his arms over his head. He arches his back and grimaces. He is tall and lean, wears a gray pajama-like onesie, the same outfit that Pancho has on. In the place where a name would be stenciled on a small rectangle on the left breast is nothing.

He walks around the room, peering into each glass-enclosed bunk. He stops at one lower bunk and touches his fingers against the glass.

"I think I love this woman."

"What woman?"

"Sleeping. Enclosed here. Beneath the glass. She must be dreaming."

"You assume she isn't horrible." Pancho cracks his back on the chair. He cradles his chin in his palm and pops his neck. "Oof. One more like that and it's over for me."

"Are you assuming she is?"

"Fifty percent chance."

"Is that all?" Lefty stands up straight and looks at the other bunks. Counts them with his finger. "Half the people in the world are good and half are horrible?"

Schuyler Dickson

"I didn't say the other half were good."

"But not horrible?"

"I remember once being in a grocery store," Pancho says. "Do you remember grocery stores?"

"I've told you all of my memories. Both of them."

"Massive buggies, narrow rows. You forget yourself for a moment while you consider all the colorful packages, maybe hold a can of beans, until someone has not grazed your hip but come so close to grazing your hip with their buggy that you become embarrassed in how easy it was to become distracted."

"I bet she has green eyes."

"And you make these tiny adjustments that do no good because the person has already passed. You move six inches and apologize, pull your buggy by the front of its cage to give a little more clearance."

"You're an inconvenience."

"I am an obstacle. And worse, you see them on the next aisle. This journey we're on, we're on together."

"Something romantic in that."

"But they despise you already. And you look at them, trying not to look at them as they look at the additives on a pickle jar, smile as you both navigate around a display that for some goddawful reason the store decides to set up in the middle of the aisle, and you realize that, yes, a piece of yourself is in love with this person, in love with all of these people, while in their eyes as you course correct your buggy is absolute detestment of you for having the gall to have a buggy so big."

"Is that why you left? Because of your difficulty reading pickle jars?"

"You are assuming I left."

"This is not a grocery store."

"It's not. And why would anyone add anything to pickles? Isn't the point of pickles that they're already preserved? How did we get here, to adding color and other things to pickles?"

"Where are we?"

"I don't know. It could be a spaceship for all I know."

"Don't know or don't recall."

"I don't remember having come."

Silence. "Me either."

"What if we embraced it?"

"Embraced our buggies?"

"Embraced our assery."

"Just say, u and me both, we're asses."

"Accept it."

"Embrace it."

"Define ourselves by our cracks."

"Exactly."

"What would that do for us?"

"We could assume things."

"It would be another tool in the toolbelt."

Schuyler Dickson

"The what?"

He searches the room. "The possibilities are endless."

"I assume that robot was faulty, if it ever occurred."

"You assume me a liar?"

"Not at all. I assume that the beings who implant memories in our heads are perhaps neither benign nor—what's the word?"

"Our thoughts may be cancerous? Is that what you're saying?"

"I think I'm done assuming for a while."

They both sit. Lefty rests his forehead in his hands. Pancho stands, moves his chair away from Lefty a bit, and sits back down. Lefty looks at him. Stands. Moves his chair closer to Pancho.

"I would like to assume that woman will wake up," Lefty says.

"Fine," Pancho says. "Let's begin with that, then."

2.

Now, atop two horses. Thinking themselves having always been on top of two horses.

Behind them, tied to a rope fastened to a saddle, they drag a coffin. The coffin has a glass window pane where the woman's face can be seen, her hair around her eyes. The desert is all around them, and in the distance small mountains loom beige but far.

"We assume she will wake up."

"Her? Absolutely not."

"We're allowing ourselves the tool of assumption, but shouldn't we assume the same thing?"

"Fair."

"She will not wake up?"

"From being dead? We are assuming she has not already woken up. In another body. Or bodiless. In another place."

"At one with the blue light."

"The what?"

"I don't know. Pretend you didn't hear me mention the blue light."

"I would have forgotten had you told me not to remember it."

"Now you'll remember it?"

"How can I forget?"

"I assume you will."

"Me too."

"Good."

"Great."

"Just by the fact that I have forgotten everything else to this point."

"Obviously."

"A safe assumption."

"If one or two were in the assumption business, that would be a grand first assumption."

"Things are looking different now, aren't they?"

"Possibly. I guess. It depends."

Schuyler Dickson

"On where one is going."

"We have to assume first that there is somewhere we are going."

Above, the birds circle. The sun is directly overhead.

"Yes. We are going somewhere."

"We are not just caught in the delusion of movement."

"Hmm."

"We have found ourselves in movement."

"Fact."

"We are moving somewhere."

"Hard to say."

"There must be a destination we are traveling to. There must have been plans put in place, else we wouldn't be dragging a coffin across the desert."

"Hmm."

"Say something besides that."

"We are assuming beyond our measure."

"She means something to us?"

"I told you I loved her."

"So she is one of us? We are burying her out of respect? We are taking her somewhere that means something to us all, a sacred place?"

"A what?"

"A sacred place."

Pancho vomits off the side of his horse.

"Is that not something we are assuming?"

"Or we were paid to track her down. She is bad news, this woman, but finding her, you have fallen in love with her."

"And I killed her anyway?"

"You hold your duty in the highest regard?"

"Or you killed her?"

"My oath is my bond."

"Or we just found her and she was dead already?"

Silence.

"Yes, it seems so."

"Why don't we just bury her right here?"

"The horses do seem tired."

One of the birds lights on the coffin. It pecks at the glass.

"All of the world has fallen in love with her."

"We don't have a shovel."

"I bet they have a shovel where we're going."

"Of course. Great."

A piece of the glass cracks.

"How much farther, do you think?"

"Oh, it can't be far."

They look around.

"The desert is full of mirages."

"We assume she's not just sleeping?"

"Why would a person sleep there?"

"She was tired of riding? Or maybe she wanted a free ride

across the sand."

"She was walking before."

"She built a coffin, knowing full well that this is not a suitable place to dig a hole."

"Why not?"

"A serious lack of shovels out here."

"Could a person not fashion one out of sand?"

"A person might. A box of potatoes? Probably not?"

"I choose to believe that we are going somewhere."

Lefty smiles at Pancho. "That's nice."

"You don't?"

"I will try. For you."

Pancho closes his eyes. He vomits off the side of the horse.

Lefty is crying. "I can't imagine. Putting my love into the sand."

"There, there."

"After all of this." Gestures around him. "After all we've been through."

"Do you remember your mother?"

"The sand is my mother. I want to assume she wakes up."

"I don't think she will."

"Try for me. Together, let's assume she wakes up. I tried for you, remember?"

"I'm not sure how much effort you put in it."

"So much I threw up. Do you not remember?"

"You could be one of those people that throws up on command. Like that friend of mine who farted on command."

"Who?"

"The story I told you. Of the friend who sucks air into his butthole."

"Some muscles I find myself having little control over."

"This is terrible."

"I agree."

"Let's assume that she wakes up. Please."

"Okay."

"Please?"

"I said okay."

Pancho closes his eyes. Lefty sees him close his eyes and closes his eyes too. They listen as the coffin slurs against the sand. The bird pecks at the glass. The bird tosses a piece of cracked glass into the air. It beaks down into the crack and tears out a piece of the woman's hair.

"It's not working," Lefty says.

"I'm having trouble."

"With what?"

"With worry. Say she does wake up. Say she remembers where we came from. Say she remembers you falling in love with her and killing her anyway. She'll want revenge."

"I imagine so."

"I don't know if we can fend her off."

"So she'll kill us. Oh well."

"Oh well?"

"Yes, oh well. Maybe that's the destination we're going to. A hole for each of us."

"No. I don't assume we'll get our own. I assume they'll throw you and me in one together."

"That would be nice."

"Then it would just keep going, wouldn't it."

Pancho vomits off the horse.

"I don't remember you eating anything."

Pancho swallows back tears and wipes his mouth with his sleeve. He snorts. "It's mostly bile."

"Suppose—no."

"What?"

"No."

"Please?"

"Well. Suppose she wakes up and doesn't remember anything at all."

"It would be horrible."

"For our sakes."

"For her sakes."

"For all our sakes."

"What would we tell her?"

"We would have a responsibility, wouldn't we?"

"I don't follow."

"We were here first. She has been sleeping. We're counted on to fill her in."

"What's there to fill in?"

"The potatoes. The coach. The decision to become an ass or not to become an ass. The composition of an ass."

"We would leave that out."

"What would we say?"

"We would say we're going somewhere."

"But we don't know that."

"But she doesn't know that."

"She would assume we knew."

"She would."

"And when we never got there?"

"You're assuming."

"That's literally what we're doing."

"It's just over the ridge, now, isn't it?"

They look back. The bird has gotten trapped in the glass. The glass has cut a hole in the bird's neck, and the bird bleeds on the glass. It squawks and flutters.

"There will be repercussions," Lefty says.

"There always are," Pancho says.

"If this woman rose from the dead, we would have to make it clear the miraculousness of that to her."

"Wouldn't she have just been sleeping, this whole time?"

"She is in a coffin. Who sleeps in coffins? Unless—"

"Yes."

"She can't be."

"I have fallen in love with a vampire?"

"No."

"And not a wooden stake in sight?"

"You would kill the woman you love again?"

"I don't think I have the option."

"She could be Christ."

"Jesus Christ sleeps in a coffin?"

"If the circumstances necessitated."

"What circumstances would make Jesus Christ sleep in a coffin?"

"Maybe not Jesus Christ. Maybe Cousin Christ sleeps in a coffin."

"You're saying now that resurrection is genetic."

"I am assuming."

"Are there no limits to our assumptions?"

"We can always go back to just the facts."

"No. No we can't. The ass is out of the bag."

"Let us assume only the best."

The bird flutters slowly and then rests.

"It is either dead or has given up."

"I said, let's assume the best."

"Oh. Okay. She has woken and is kissing the bird."

"Is that the best? Your love wakes up and chooses not just

someone else but shows a hankering for the bestial?"

"I'm no good at this."

"Sure you are."

"No. We never should have started assuming."

"It has been really good for us. No doubt about it."

"You think?"

"Where would we be without it?"

Lefty looks around.

"Don't say it."

"I couldn't."

"Not that you would remember if you did."

"No. At least there's that."

"That's a great idea. Let's count our blessings."

"Our what?"

"Be grateful, they say."

"Who says? Who are you talking about?"

"It's like priming the pump. The more grateful you are, the more things you'll find to be grateful for."

They look around.

Pancho's horse collapses.

3.

"The thought just occurred to me," Pancho says, "that I have no control over which thoughts occur to me."

"Yes."

"And if an action is preceded by a thought, and a thought is not preceded by a conscious trigger, then what?"

"Exactly."

"Then I am not the one doing the action that I think that I am doing? If not me, then who? Who is causing me to have these thoughts? Or what?"

"Uh-huh."

"Are you listening to me?"

"I am not."

"Please. This is important. This whole time, my decision to assume or not to assume itself was an assumption. I was assuming that I was making a decision."

"Of course."

"Do you follow me?"

"Please. I'm just trying to follow my own thoughts for a while. Just for a while. A little quiet would be nice."

"But this is important."

"It's all important. When is it ever not important?"

"I'm close to understanding it all."

"So fine. You've understood it. Leave me alone about it."

"But I need help. I need someone to hear me."

"And what about me? Don't I need some quiet time? Every now and then? How am I supposed to know where my thoughts come from if you never let me have one?"

"So you were listening?"

"Of course I was listening! What is there to do but always listen to you go on and on? I have no choice but to listen to you."

"Yes. That's exactly it. If a person has no control over the thoughts in his or her own head, then what is the source of those thoughts?"

"Okay."

"Please."

"I said okay."

"But who says okay. You had a thought to say okay. But where did the thought come from? It just appeared, did it not? And it could have been any thought at all. It could have been you saying okay. It could have been you saying no. It could have been an image of a topless woman on the beach."

"That would have been nice. Why do you do that to me? Why do you show me how much better my thoughts could have been?"

"I'm trying to understand why it is that I don't constantly see myself and think of myself surrounded by topless women at the beach? Wouldn't that be nice? Wouldn't that be better than—whatever it is that this is?"

"What is the question?"

"What is the source of our thoughts?"

"You're making an assumption that there is a source."

"Yes. I am. That's what we're doing. We're making assumptions."

"I've gotten tired of it. Let's go back to the topless beach."

"We've never been to a topless beach."

"We were never invited?"

"We were cast out at the gates."

"Well. The uppity gatekeepers of the topless beach. I'll have a word or two for them."

"Yes. Good. And where will those words come from?"

"What does it matter?"

"Just assume it matters."

"Where are we now?"

"The void. As always. Now please."

"Where do our thoughts come from, that's the question?"

"Yes."

"You've pulled me away from the topless beach to ask me where thoughts come from?"

"I have."

"Well then. Okay. We are assuming they come from somewhere. In that they are caused."

"Yes."

"And it appears clear that that cause, even though many believe and we believed for a very long time that that cause was ourselves, is not our conscious minds."

"Yes. Very good. Thank you for being with me."

"And if we figure this out, they will let us picnic for eternity on the topless beach."

"Absolutely."

"Where no one cares if you ogle."

"Or dawdle."

"Or diddle."

"Or fiddle."

"Well, then. The sooner we begin, the sooner we can get to fiddling."

"Glad to have you on board."

"So the question is where our thoughts come from."

"Yes."

"And the assumption is that our thoughts come from somewhere as opposed to just appearing fully formed in our brains out of nowhere."

"That is the assumption."

"That there is a causative event or substance."

"Or event and substance."

"Because it's pretty clear to me now that you've walked me through it and especially now that we have a clear goal in mind that a person does not cause his own thoughts. They just occur. If I want to be a diddler or a dawdler, I sit in the darkness and pretend to think until out of the darkness an answer comes: a diddler you will be. So my first answer would be that thoughts come as a response from our environment."

"Thoughts pop up and here we were claiming credit for them. That's our argument. By the way, who is it that is keeping us from dawdling at the beach?"

"I don't know. One might imagine it is the same event and substance that is the source of our thoughts."

"And the Source is mad that we've been taking credit all these years."

"It expects confession."

"Restitution."

"Penitence."

"Self-flagellation."

"Tearing of beards."

"We must find the source of our thoughts and present to it the source of our inadequacy."

"One is the gate keeper and one is the key master."

"Wouldn't the sand get sticky?"

"Not following."

"You know. All the fiddling."

"The sand turns to glass."

"Interesting."

"The beach is practically a glass factory. It's how they can afford all that sunscreen."

"I did not know that."

"There you go."

"But listen. We did not choose our environment, either, unless a thought before coming to this environment chose this environment, but we did not choose that thought that chose that environment, either. If a person's surroundings, where he or she chooses to go, is caused by the thoughts in his or her head, then saying that thoughts are caused by environment gives us a kind of snake eating its own tail type of situation here I'm thinking. Where did you say we are again?"

"The thought occurred to me that we are two germs inside the guts of a bird but there's no way to say for sure really."

"And at some point, this was part of the plan?"

"I know of no plan."

"We thought it beneficial at some point to become two germs in the belly of a bird. And here I'm using 'we' as not our thoughts but the 'we' beneath our thoughts, the we that is both gate keeper and key master and that desires nothing more than to watch us sitting side by side on the topless beach, slathering ourselves with complementary sunscreen, not a drop of liquid left in our bodies so as it is difficult to even blink any more, surrounded by glass that I'm guessing robots or maybe sea birds come to collect and package and ship and all those capitalistic logistics that keep the tits and wieners out."

"We must have. Or else the plan was made without our consent."

"Or we made the plan and hid it from ourselves."

"Ouch."

"What?"

"I think there may be ants in here."

"Scootch this way."

"Oh my god they're everywhere."

Schuyler Dickson

"Scootch. Scootch scootch scootch."

"I am scootching. There is nowhere to scootch where there are not ants. Oh my god they're eating my skin."

"I'm not in ants. Scootch near me."

"I don't see you."

"Follow the sound of my voice. I'll keep talking so you can have some direction."

"I can't see you."

"Oh no."

"What? The ants got you too? Am I heading into more ants?"

"My love. I do not see her."

"You wouldn't. Not in the dark."

"It is as if ants are eating my soul."

"We are both afflicted. Mine is actual."

"Let's not compete in our suffering."

"Why not? You think you might lose?"

"Don't you do it. Not for one more second. Competition is a pleasure we can't afford. Winning will never get you to The Fiddling Dunes."

"The bites are almost pleasurable sometimes. If one doesn't pay attention to being devoured."

"That's the spirit. Do you think, though, the beach could be both topless and bottomless?"

"Oh, absolutely."

"I'd like to see cracks."

"Cracks as far as you can see."

"Well good. Let's continue, then. Would you mind not slapping your skin so loudly?"

"I can't help it. They're everywhere."

"I understand. I'm just having trouble thinking."

"They're in my mouth. I think they're crawling down my throat."

"Swallow really hard and your stomach acid should take care of them. Although, it'll be tough to swallow that these ants don't do much for either your void or your bird theory. Get it? Tough to swallow?"

"I'm dying."

"No, I imagine we're in some kind of cave. Ah well. No way to know. The beach will be right out the mouth of the cave, I'd imagine. Are you there? Are you listening to me?"

"I'm trying not to scream."

"We've talked about this. It's hard for me to talk and then you not listen. It's why I stay silent so much of the time."

"My whole body will soon be a colony."

"There you go."

"What good is suffering if it's not displayed?"

"Do you ever feel assaulted by your own thoughts? Not necessarily the content, but the frequency?"

"You're comparing your thoughts to my ants."

"You own them now?"

"There is much of me in them."

"I'm getting tired of this."

"You want to stop?"

"I don't know."

"It's fine to stop."

"I don't know what that would look like."

"It's probably a bad assumption."

"What is?"

"That if we figure out where our thoughts come from then they'll let us go to the beach."

"We're assuming we're not at the beach right now."

"This is the void."

"We're assuming there is another place that we are capable of getting to in which our cares and desires are all totally extinguished and/or fulfilled at the moment in which they appear so that we get to have both desire and fulfillment maybe not simultaneously but in a very short amount of time. And we have set ourselves a goal that we think, if we accomplish it, will grant us access to the land where our desires are constantly and forever met in a very short amount of time after the desires show themselves."

"Desires which we have no control over."

"Right."

"Which we do not choose but rather are subjected to."

"Yes. And because we have thoughts, through no fault of our own, that there is another place where the thoughts that we think are more harmonious with the place in which we think them, that that situation has made this place that we're in, which is fine, otherwise intolerable because this place is not that place."

"It's fine?"

"And we are making the assumption that even if we get to that place, that we will not tire of that place and create, in our heads—"

"—through no thought or control of our own—"

"—a desire to be another place entirely, thus turning that beach where we diddle and fiddle without end or consequence into another type of hell."

"One might tire of the ass cracks on that beach and want another beach."

"Ass cracks of different lengths or widths. How are your ants, by the way?"

"They are delighting in my arteries."

"Your body is the beach of the ants."

"I have become a planet."

"That seems like something the gatekeepers should know."

4.

Now is a burning forest.

Now is a bad guy kicked off a skyscraper.

Now is a truck on a gravel road.

Now is the birth of a baby god.

Schuyler Dickson

Now is the Senate hearing on Consciousness.

Now is an octopus resting.

Now the doctor will see you.

Now is an exploding sun.

Now it's time for the money shot.

Now the elephants are mourning.

Now the idea is gone.

Now the magic wand is broken.

Now it's not much longer.

Now we're cooking with oil.

Now is a building collapsing.

Now is a wind howling.

Now the bomb is ticking.

Now is a flower blooming.

5.

Now is a funeral home. Thick purple-pink carpet and plastic folding chairs in rows. All smells of stale perfume. Near the altar is an open casket. Along the walls are circular windows, out of which space and stars track by.

"Are we not the heroes?" Pancho asks.

"I don't think so," Lefty says. "But would you say we're the bad guys?"

"I don't even think I would give us that."

"We have nothing to set ourselves against."

"Nothing but ourselves."

"Could we assume ourselves in communion with all?"

"We would have to assume there is such thing as all."

"Something other than us."

"A big assumption. Whether all that we experience is ourselves or separate from ourselves."

"If it is an either/or at all. Could there not be a hemisphere in which the world is both us, at times, and not us, at times."

"Or if there is a hemisphere between me and you."

"Or then and now."

"Or now and will be."

"Or this and that."

"How would one begin to assume?"

"Have we not begun already?"

"From what are we assuming?"

"Just the facts, ma'am."

"At this point, I'm afraid we'll never make it to the bottomless beach."

"Are you in despair?"

"I think so."

"There, there. It's okay. Put your head on my shoulder. Let me comfort you."

"I'd like to stop assuming for a little while."

"Wow."

"What?"

"Nothing. It's okay."

"No. What?"

"Your hair is pungent."

"Please don't insult me while I'm in despair."

"I'm sorry. Let's stop assuming for a little while."

"Okay. Yes. That's fine."

"I will state the facts as I know them."

"That would be comforting. And you know what else would be comforting?"

"What?"

"It's a little much to ask."

"You can ask. You're in despair and I want to help."

"Could you sing them to me?"

"You would like me to sing the facts to you? I would have to make a new song."

"You can use an old song. No one is here."

"No one besides us."

"If we even count as ones. I am despairing and degenerating and feel so very far from the beach that is both topless and bottomless and, now that I think of it, probably sandless too."

"Shh. It's okay. I'll sing to you everything we know. Would that make you feel better?"

"I guess."

"Do you have a melody you prefer? I can't think of one offhand."

"I've never known any melodies."

"I'm afraid you may not like my voice."

"You value your dignity more than you want to comfort me?"

"Ah hah. I have it. I'll whisper sing it. Like you're a baby."

"If that's what you have to do."

"Perfect. We'll do 'Rock-a-bye Baby,' unless you'd prefer Boyz II Men's 'End of the Road.'"

"My despair only increases. Rock-a-Bye."

"Fine. Fine. Shush." Clears throat. "Okay. Alright. We don't—Is it okay if I don't rhyme? I don't have the mental capacity or the desire really to make this rhyme. Is that going to ruin it for you?"

"All is ruined."

"Ah. Good. So this will be one more among many. Great. Put your head on my shoulder."

Clears throat.

"We don't know where our thoughts come from

We didn't choose where we are

We don't control where we go

And we don't remember where we've been."

"I remember some."

"You interrupted me?"

"I remember some of where we've been. The robots. The coach."

"And we don't remember ninety-nine percent of where we've

Schuyler Dickson

been. Is that better?"

"Yes."

"Every moment we are assailed

From inside and out, none of which we control

We make assumptions to make it make sense

And when the stories fall apart, we come back right here.

Here is fine, but we have desires,

and we imagine a place where all desires come true

And thinking of that place makes this place intolerable

Then we suffer despair and sing a song to recover."

Silence.

"I feel much better now. Thank you."

"Were you disgusted by my singing voice?"

"Not really."

"What do you want to do now?"

"I don't know."

Lefty stands up from the chair and walks down the aisle toward the coffin. He cries, his back spasming in short breaths.

"Have you decided to leave me?" Pancho asks.

Lefty shakes his head. "I was worried you were revolted by my hair smell," he says through the tears.

"I was just coming to tolerate it. Admire it, in some ways."

"The song," Lefty says. "You left her out of it."

"I didn't know what to say."

"Yes you do. You just didn't want to. Go ahead. Say it."

"I don't think she's going to wake up."

"That's an assumption."

"It is."

"And you're assuming, too, that she hasn't already woken up somewhere else. That she hasn't joined the place where all souls congregate and then delight in existence as its shorn from all its vestments before choosing another scenario in which to better learn from the mistakes of the past life in a permanent, cosmic trip where we all are being drawn to the singular great creator who exists in us all even now, who is the source of every thought and experience of creating itself out of itself and drawing itself home again."

"Into the blue light."

"Yes. The blue light." Lefty reaches into the coffin and takes the woman's hand. "She's beautiful. Do you think she was our mother?"

"I don't know. I don't know anything."

"Do you think she loved us?"

"I don't know."

"Could we assume she did?"

"Sure. If you want to. We can do whatever you want."

"I know that. Could we assume she can communicate with us, from wherever she is?"

"I don't know."

"You said we can do whatever we want."

"I did. Okay. Sure. I'm sorry. Yes."

"What is she saying?"

"What?"

"She is talking through you. What is she saying?"

"I don't know."

"You said we could do this. You said so. Please. What is she saying?"

"Okay." Deep breath. "She says she loves us."

"What else?"

"I don't know. Please let's do something else."

"No. What else?"

Pancho sighs and cradles his head in his hands. "She says she is the source of our thoughts."

"It was her? All along? She was the source and then she sent us on a quest to find the source? That trickster. She is such a rascal, isn't she?"

"She says we were detectives all along, I guess."

"Just the facts, ma'am. Say that to her. See if she laughs."

"Just the facts, ma'am."

"Did she laugh?"

"I don't know."

"What else does she say? Ask her if she's going to wake up."

"She says no."

"Oh. Well. Ask her if we're going to see her soon."

"If we want to."

"Wow. What does that mean? That all along, we haven't

wanted to?"

"I don't know."

"I guess we see her right now, don't we?"

"I suppose so."

"Ask her if we can go to the beach next."

"She says sure."

"Maybe the water will heal our bites."

"She says she's tired. She says she needs to go."

"Oh. Yes, of course."

"She says goodbye. And that she loves us."

"We love her, too. Tell her we love her, too."

"She knows. She says goodbye."

Silence.

"Thank you," Lefty says.

Pancho nods.

"I'm tired now. Can we be done assuming for a while?"

"Yes. Absolutely."

"Could I rest my head in your lap?"

Pancho sits up straight and pats his thigh. Lefty lies across the folding chairs. Rests his head on Pancho's lap.

"Would you sing a song to me while I try to sleep?"

"I only know the one."

"That one's fine. I enjoyed it earlier."

"You don't think you'll grow tired of it?"

"I don't know. Hey. Maybe I'll have another memory when I

wake up."

"Maybe so."

Pancho sings.

Schuyler Dickson is a writer and regenerative farmer. He earned a BA in Southern Studies from Ole Miss and his MFA in Creative Writing from Northwestern, where he won the Distinguished Thesis Award. His stories have appeared in **JMWW, Split Lip Magazine, PANK, and New World Writing,** among others. He lives with his wife and children in Houlka, MS, and can be found at schuylerdickson.com.